STREETS OF GOLD

STREETS OF GOLD

Contemporary Glasgow Stories

edited by

MOIRA BURGESS
and
HAMISH WHYTE

MAINSTREAM PUBLISHING

First published in Great Britain in 1989 by
MAINSTREAM PUBLISHING CO. (EDINBURGH) LTD.
7 Albany Street
Edinburgh EH1 3UG

ISBN 1 85158 237 1 (cloth)
ISBN 1 85158 242 8 (paper)

BRN

51130

The publisher acknowledges subsidy of the Scottish Arts Council
towards the publication of this volume.

British Library Cataloguing in Publication Data

Streets of gold.
1. Short stories in English, 1945 — Anthologies
I. Burgess, Moira, 1936- II. White, Hamish
823'.9'.1 [FS]

ISBN 1-85158-237-1
ISBN 1-85158-2427-8 Pbk

Reproduced from disc 10/12 Baskerville by
Polyprint, 48 Pleasance, Edinburgh EH8 9TJ.

Printed in Great Britain by
Billings & Sons Ltd, Worcester.

Contents

Introduction

In our earlier volume of Glasgow stories, *Streets of Stone*, the editorial policy was fairly firm: for inclusion a story had to be set in Glasgow, truthfully depicting some aspect of Glasgow life or expressing some essential trait of Glasgow character. There was also a historical dimension in that the stories were gathered from fifty years of writing, from the nineteen-thirties to the early nineteen-eighties. In *Streets of Gold*, while we have not lost sight of these criteria, there is no such mission. We have selected stories this time all by contemporary writers, demanding only that they have some connection with Glasgow — either by birth, upbringing, residence, or context or setting of work. The stories have been written within the last ten years (some published here for the first time, most of them previously uncollected in book form) and are offered as characteristic of their authors. Chronologically, in terms of setting, they range from the no-particular-time of fantasy to historical events this century, from the present or recent past to bleak visions of the future.

Another point of contrast with *Streets of Stone* worth noting might be the increased representation of women writers in the present collection (nine as opposed to three in the earlier book). One thing remains the same — both collections feature work by well-known writers together with those still to make their mark.

Glasgow is the official European City of Culture for 1990. "Everywhere in this city culture, eh?" observes a character in one of the stories, though we leave it to the reader to savour the beauty of his remark in its particular context. The setting and subject of some of the stories (France, art, music, etc.) might seem appropriate to this event, but the main aim of the

7

anthology is to reflect the current creativity of Glasgow in the field of fiction, to reflect the life of the city, culture with a big or a wee c — to provide a sample-book of Glasgow writing of the 1980s.

Moira Burgess
Hamish Whyte
February 1989

SUSAN CAMPBELL

Agape

I was staring out the smoky windows, watching the charred tenement-faces slip by, their broken eyes and gaping door-mouths. The bus was for some reason intact, though the driver was half-dead, flopped over the wheel like a question mark. A large, round, yellow man cavorted along the outside, smirking behind his hand, pronouncing in thick black letters, "GLASGOW'S MILES BETTER". Inside there was only me and my friend Chrissie up the front, and a lot of derelicts slumped in the back seats, missing their stop every time round and round in circles. So Chrissie my pal was going he said and SHE said, and wait till you hear, and patting me on the arm with her flippery hand, what with her sense of drama, when, from up my sleeve, rolling on to my raincoat lap, appeared the ring. It sat there, chucking light about, and my heart flopped over like a big caught fish. Then the ring was in my hand and in my pocket and Chrissie was still going she said he said and as the fish ceased its assault on my rib cage I looked up to find the burned-out eyes in the driving-mirror fixed on me.

So I had a think. Twenty minutes before, right, I was standing in a shop, gawping, with all these racks of fluffy jumpers and lead-lined suits, and the dried-up plants and bare girders, and the two lassies going haw haw etc. at the far end, when I saw that ring, sitting on its pedestal, with its glass dome on the floor beside it. I thought, better tell they lassies before some chancer takes a fancy to that. But then I thought, hang on. My Kev is up to his oxters in fornication, thinking I don't know. Cannae afford a ring to please her expensive Bearsden taste and make it decent, and the minister thinking I cannae

9

bring my kid up right. Here's ma chance. I'll do a wee wrong thing and prevent a greater evil.

But then I thought, no, two wrongs make double trouble, as my Mam used to say.

But then I thought, seeing as I'm one of the Underprivileged, my husband terminally unemployed, people spraying Nuke The Pope on my lobby etcetera, why should I not get a wee free gift for a change, seeing as it's not for me.

But then I thought, stealing's a sin however you look at it, and I'll burn in Hell, and all of a bustle I turned and nearly ran out and up to the bus-stop before I could change my mind, my skin hot and crawling, and there I met Chrissie with her hesaid shesaid and here I find the thing had got itself stuck up my sleeve somehow.

So there was a different game, and I sat there on the bus, mulling it over. Was it stealing if something fell into my lap? Or was the ring meant to save Kevin from the big fire? The bus stopped at a traffic light and a wee boy shouted EVEnin' TIAMS from the pavement. He was sitting, legless, on a trolley and his newsboard said OUTRAGE in huge print, and I thought this ring could be a tiny link in God's plan. A man in an overcoat came up and shoved the boy round the corner and started hawking an inflatable dome with free mask. The bus moved off, not that the lights had changed, since they'd all been broken for days, and I thought to myself, mibbe I passed a wee test back there, seeing I didn't take it, and this is my reward. I was getting fond of that one too, till we reached our stop, and as we got off that old driver opened one ashy eye to give me a wink, and I felt my guilt kindle, and knew then that my thought was sinful. We crossed the wasteland, stepping over the rubble where the tenements had been, and the guys lying there in heaps, stinking to heaven, and by the time I'd said goodnight to Chrissie and watched her hirple off, and climbed the stairs, skirting the sodden bundles slumped about the landings, I'd made up my mind to take it back.

Kevin was out, and Peter, my husband, was sitting in his chair saying nothing as usual, so I put the TV on and made him his tea, and by the time I sat down it was the News and

Shock Horror the enemy was approaching and thousands were dead in the streets and that, just like every night, and my mind wouldn't stay on what I was watching but kept on wandering back to the ring in my raincoat pocket in the cupboard. So finally, even though it was getting dark, I thought I'd take my life in my hands and walk along to the church for some of that spiritual sustenance to keep me right. Off I goes, buttoned into my raincoat, making Peter a cup of tea first, and one of the biscuits to keep him quiet, and as I was crossing the wasteland, I saw this shell of a car, black and buckled with fire, the top gaping, the wheel-sockets empty. Far from the streetlights and it was all dusk and drizzle and dodgy underfoot with the stray animals but something or other made me swerve from the way I was going and make towards the car, and as I got closer I saw inside the shadows locked and heaving. I went right up to it, looked in the broken top, and there was Kevin and his trollop making the beast with two backs over the bare springs of the front seats. She was going him like a racing bike and my wee boy staring up at the sky with a dead look in his eye, and his mother with her face tripping her. I made not a sound but backed off to walk quietly home again. Oh but my insides had hardened and I knew then what the something or other was that led me to the car on my way to the church to show me what to do. To save them from this unholy coupling, like dogs in the debris, I was to give him the ring in the morning.

But by the time I'd got Peter up and sat him in his chair and organised him, Kevin had slunk off to the site, crook-eyed, close-mouthed, never giving me the chance to have a word. It would keep till teatime, or so I thought. But when I'd done the dishes and went to tidy the shelter under the stairs, there on the floor was the Good Book, lying open. Peter, for reasons best known to himself, had been reading it there in the night, the deep one. I picked it up and looked at the face it presented. The Sermon On The Mount. I dropped it and a dead black bird fluttered to the spiralled carpet. Thou Shalt Not Steal! Heed the Word, thought I, especially when it's squawked in your ear, and I went to get my coat with its little-lumpy pocket. On my way out I patted Peter goodbye and he crumbled into a heap of ashes. Not touched for too long.

Toiled across the wasteland, clutching my pocket to keep faith, the dirty yellow metal sky a great dome, like inside an eggshell, with all around the broken horizon. As I laboured forward towards the city the dust and filth was rising in a cloud and the yellow sky went black and the weak old sun was blotted out, and as I crossed the road to the shop, I was hit by a bloody great bus. As I performed a graceless somersault, I beheld in my dead shadow, spreading on the concrete, a bug-eyed beastie, fallen broken-winged, clinging to the tilt of the turning world, eyes and mouth open to the heavens, expectant, agape. Fast and huge below me it ballooned. I landed, it splattered, and here I find myself, my crushed limbs arranged, being goggled at by masked faces. Salt water mingles with blood in my mouth, wide with praise and wonder that I live. The masked faces float by, sea-monsters in the thick air, and now the sirens begin to wail.

MICHAEL MUNRO

Application

The kettle switched itself off the boil with a sharp click. The young man filled the teapot with the steaming water and dropped in a teabag to succour the one already there. He sat the full pot on the formica-topped breakfast bar and made a silly face at his five-year-old daughter who was perched on a stool slowly getting through a bowl of milky porridge. Hearing his wife coming down the stairs from the bathroom he began to refill her mug but instead of entering the bright warm kitchen she lingered in the hall. He could hear her pulling on her heavy coat. She came in saying she had no time, she'd be late for her lift, her heels clattering on the tiled floor. She kissed goodbye to daughter and husband then was off in a whirl of newly-applied perfume and the swish of her clothes and the front door slamming.

He sat down on his stool and poured himself another mug of tea. He asked the child how she was doing, was the porridge too hot? She told him gravely that it was OK and went on making a show of blowing on each hot spoonful as she had been shown.

He picked up the newspaper that was lying folded open at the Situations Vacant pages. One advert was targeted in a ring of red felt-tip pen. The come-on was in big bold italics: *"This time last year I was made redundant. Now I own a £50,000 house, drive a BMW and holiday in Bali. If you . . ."* He opened out the paper and refolded it to the front page to check the headlines. The date he knew already but there it was plain and remorseless: exactly one year he had been out of work.

13

Father and daughter chatted brightly as they strolled hand in hand down Allison Street heading for school. She was a talkative child and he would egg her on in her prattle for his own amusement. It was now well into the rush hour: traffic gushed by or fretted at red lights and urgent pedestrians commanded the pavements and crossings. It was bitter cold. He looked down at the girl to reassure himself that she was warmly enough dressed, but there was no need; he was well used to getting her ready. Her round reddened face was the only prey to the cold air and she beamed up at him, quite content.

At the last corner before the school's street they both halted in an accustomed way and he squatted down to give her a kiss. She didn't mind the daily ritual but forbade its enactment outside the gates: her pals might see and that would be too embarrassing. He tugged her knitted hat a little further down her forehead and tucked in a couple of strands of her long reddish hair. They could hear the kids' voices laughing and shouting from the playground. They waved cheerio at the gate and he stood watching until she was inside and assumed into some little coterie, then he turned away. He was vaguely aware of one or two mothers doing likewise and one or two car doors slamming. With both gloveless hands shoved into the pockets of his cream-coloured raincoat he made for home. Behind him the bell began to sound above and through the high excited voices.

He finished writing the letter and signed his name with a brisk underline, printing it in brackets below, just in case. Picking up the CV from the coffee table he glanced over its familiar outlines. It looked good, he thought, organised, businesslike. His wife had managed to get a couple of dozen of them run off on her word processor at the office. It was the contents that struck him as pointless. What use was it to anyone to know what he had done at school? It was the grown man, someone with work experience, who was on offer, not the schoolboy. Not the kid who'd scuffed along, neither brilliant nor stupid, not the football-daft apprentice smoker and opportunist drinker who'd put his name to those long-forgotten exam papers then sauntered out carefree into the world. Well, maybe not carefree: he could still remember some of the burdens and terrors of adolescence that he'd laugh at now, the state he was in now. Then there was his five years of selling for the one firm. No problem there; those were good years. Their fruits were holidays abroad, marriage, the house, the baby. Plain sailing until the company had gone bust. Now he was no longer classifiable as young and upwardly mobile. Not even horizontally mobile: stopped, stuck.

Referees. He always wanted to write "Tiny Wharton" but didn't. What did people expect to hear from the names he always supplied — "Don't touch this character, he's a definite no-user"? It was just wee games, this form-filling. He believed it was the interview that would count, if only he could land one.

He ranged the letter and CV together, tapping sides and tails until there was no overlap, then folded them in half and in half again. The envelope was ready, briskly typed by his wife this morning on the old manual machine she used for home typing jobs. As he made ready to lick the stamp he stopped suddenly. Damn! He'd done it again, folding the sheets in half twice. That was clumsy, unprofessional-looking. The way she'd shown him was much better: folding one third then another so that you only had two folds instead of three. Gingerly, he tried to reopen the envelope but it was stuck fast and the flap ripped jaggedly. He'd have to type another one himself in his laborious two-fingered style. He knew he should practise, try to work up some speed and fluency, but he could never face it and always made excuses to his wife and himself for finding other things to do.

His first go had two mistakes and he was painting them over with correcting fluid when it struck him how the white stuff glared reproachfully from the buff envelope. He typed another one, slowly, making sure he got everything right. The CV was no problem, plenty of spares, but the letter would have to be written out again. He didn't hesitate, just took out a clean sheet and smoothed it down.

He kept walking, on past the pillar-box at the corner of their street. That one was definitely unlucky: nothing he had ever offered there had brought good fortune. No, he would carry on to Victoria Road whose business and air of industry made it feel a more hopeful point of departure. As he reached the main thoroughfare he saw a mailvan pull up at the post-box he was heading for and he quickened pace out of his saunter. He watched the grey-uniformed driver jump down and unlock the red door; he broke into a run. Disembowelled, the pillar-box yielded a bulky flow of mail to the driver's hand combing it into his big shapeless bag. The young man handed over his letter with a half-smile although his heart had sunk. One letter in all that flow of paper. And how many were job applications piled randomly, meaninglessly on top of one another? His own would soon be lost in that anonymous crowd. It seemed to him now more than ever like buying a raffle ticket, like backing the coupon every week. What chance had you got?

The red van nosed purposefully out into the mid-morning traffic. Plenty of work for the Post Office anyway. Maybe he could get taken on at Christmas. Christmas! He tried not to think about it but it loomed in the back of his mind like the threat of nuclear war. His digital watch told him, among other things, that he had plenty of time for a walk in Queen's Park before the school came out for lunch.

He stumped up the steep tree-shadowed paths towards the summit of Camp Hill, up towards the flagpole. He was concentrating on keeping his footing on the slippery skin of dead brown leaves; his shoes had long since lost their grip. Doing this climb nearly every day had made him feel rather fitter than he used to be. When he'd had the company car his wife would say that he wouldn't walk the length of himself. Fitness was a vogue commodity now, but fit for what? It took a different sort of stamina, the race he was in, round and round in circles till you drop. He was aware of his breath vapouring out in front of him. Maybe the Campsies would have snow on them today.

A big mongrel dog came bouncing towards him, checked in a slither of leaves and claws and came to sniff him enthusiastically. He patted its damp head and laughingly tried to keep its muddy paws off his raincoat. He looked up at the sound of a displeased voice calling the animal to heel. A middle-aged man in a blue car-coat stood there shaking his head resignedly. The young man smiled, said it was OK, he liked dogs. The older man smiled back and paused as if willing to chat. He'd seen him around the park before; he must be early retired or redundant. But the dog was off, crashing through the rhododendrons and its owner cursed half-heartedly, winked and called a farewell before hurrying after his charge.

Within the railed circle at the flagpole the young man encountered only a couple of boys sharing a bench and a cigarette. They should have been at school at this hour. One wore a multicoloured sweater with an expensive brand name. The other had on a light summer jacket, sleeves pushed up to the elbows, and his hands and forearms were red with the cold. They allowed the stranger a dispassionate brief glance before lapsing back into their casually obscene conversation.

The view was a disappointment today. Northwards the edges of the city and the hills he knew to lie beyond were erased by grey walls of mist that merged upward into low cloud. He could just make out the Cathedral's green roof straight ahead and the University's spires off to the west. Victoria Road ran arrow-straight for the city's heart. He could hear, distant, all around, the sound of the city and it seemed to him like the vague roar of a titanic air-conditioner. He watched the cars and buses and lorries bleed in and outward on the main roads.

It was easy now to recall the bustle of business life. Now it was just about lunchtime, when offices and shops would exchange populations with the pubs and restaurants. He could picture his former colleagues about their business lunches: the customers and clients, the mugs and suckers and flymen; the mates, alliances, conspiracies and flirtations, stories and jokes, continental lager and curries and games of squash. He could see their flushed faces, triumphant, sated. It was something to think about: all this unemployment and the town still buzzed with a life that would not be quelled. It came to him how much he wanted it, that activity. It was more than just something you did to make money: it was the only life he knew and he was missing out on it, standing on the sidelines like a face in the crowd at a football game. If it wasn't for the child, he thought, he wouldn't have the will to keep on trying.

He checked his watch again: the kids would soon be coming out.

He waited at their corner. 'hands deep in pockets, his shoulder to the dirty grey sandstone wall. The bell was ringing and he could hear the children streaming out into the playground. When she spotted him she broke into a trot and he retreated round the corner a little to swoop suddenly with a mock roar, bearing her laughing wildly up into his arms. As he set her down he asked quite formally what kind of morning she'd had. She began to speak, a child's narrative of rushing and halting and her enthusiasm breathed upwards into his smiling face and beyond in the chill air.

Berth

The 19.10 Cathcart Outer Circle clattered away from Glasgow Central over the Clyde. It was dark and slightly misty but the Christmas fairy lights strung between the masts of the *Carrick* and along the quayside were visible.

The two men in the almost empty rear coach swayed in unison, like the dummy lovebirds in that Hitchcock film. They had been drinking and some slurred conversation could be heard above the noise of the wheels.

"I'll miss you."

"Don't be —"

"I've no excuse now. I know it's your birthday tomorrow. Your room'll be empty, I'll just nip down, leave a card and a wee present. Shouldny tell you — it's a key ring."

"Och, don't —"

"I might," leaning with the train into confidence, "move into your room, it's more private like. Bring the girlfriend for a wee session, couple cans lager, you know, a wee bit sex. . . . You were my excuse."

The men got up too early for Queen's Park and lurched unsailorlike to the doors. The train stopped, the doors slid open and they staggered out on to the platform.

"Zis the right one?" They peered at a notice.

The station was in the throes of refurbishment. Some of the lights were out, making the place even more gloomy. A broken rocking horse lay on a pile of rubble. Pages from the day before's *Daily Record* made a crazy paving near the Victoria Road exit.

"Never trample on the printed word," one of the men said.

They side-stepped together, brothers in the routine: daft, suddenly dainty, as if drunkenness was a state of grace.

LORN MACINTYRE

Black Cherries

My great-aunt Kirsty died, aged eighty-eight, in the Blessed Heart Nursing Home, Glasgow, last year. Not that she was Catholic; her husband Tommy had been a shareholder in Rangers football team. But Kirsty seemed to feel safer with the Sisters; the odour of sanctity mixed with disinfectant?

It was an expensive place to end her days — four hundred a week, and that didn't include the physiotherapy to try and get movement back into an arm at least after the stroke. I visited her once. There was a peephole in the door so that the nuns could keep an eye on her without disturbing her. The room had quality fittings, a private bathroom she couldn't reach. You couldn't make out what she was saying.

To finance herself in the home she'd sold her Clarkston house to an insurance company in a complicated deal that would let her go on occupying it for the rest of her life. She never got home. There was enough capital left to convey her in some style to the south side cemetery, and then, after a proper interval, to add her name to Tommy's ostentatious stone.

I was left the contents of the Clarkston house. After Tommy's death (a coronary; he was pushing seventeen stones), she'd decanted from a twelve-roomed place on Great Western Road, looking straight into the Botanic Gardens, to this four apartment semi-detached bungalow. The best pieces had had to go under the hammer because they'd never have gone in the new door. (Tommy had twenty suits and yards of shoes.) There had been some good pictures, some bought abroad, but they had to be sold when Tommy's business began to go.

21

I was glad to get a couple of hundred from a second-hand man to clear the place, but I kept some of the personal effects. At one time Tommy had been one of the richest men in Glasgow. Not of the Burrell class (who was?) but loaded enough to go abroad every year with Kirsty.

There were dozens of albums of photographs, but I hadn't the space or the interest. My side of the family had never really approved of Kirsty's marriage, since Tommy had the reputation of being a crook. It's a pity I wasn't able to identify some of the people in the photos: my mother says that Kirsty claimed to have helped make the Riviera fashionable, and had seen Scott Fitzgerald water-skiing.

In Kirsty's bureau drawer I came across a marble-coloured exercise book. *Black Cherries* was written in fancy italics on the flyleaf. I thought it was a recipe book, but something made me flick through it.

It was an old cash-book, but the debits and credits columns had been used as a diary for 1927. *At Port Vendres.* It had been heavily corrected, with question marks and "no, that's not right" written in different inks in the margin.

It was always known in the family that Kirsty could have done better for herself. Her postcards (before my time) were the kind you kept. I suspect that Kirsty left this diary, to see what I would do with it. Put it into the black sack with the other stuff, share papers of Tommy's long since cashed in?

When I started publishing short stories, then a novel, she wrote me a note, saying she was following my career with interest, and that we must have a chat sometime. Instead, she left me her story *Black Cherries* to destroy or get published. My changes are minor.

At Port Vendres: Sunday 22nd May 1927

Our third night; only the menu's changed. He's sitting in his corner. I have never seen finer, whiter hands on a man. He tugs a black cherry from the stalk, splits it with the blade, then puts half into his mouth. He holds the other half between thumb and forefinger, as if he's offering it to the empty chair opposite. Then he closes his eyes and eats both halves very slowly.

What a sad face. Has his wife left him? That's what I said to Tommy before we came down to dinner. The name Hôtel du Commerce gives it away. Of course we could afford something much better, but I want *atmosphere*. (This place reminds me of the boarding-house Mummy used to take us to at Rothesay; a room filled with the tang of sea.)

I smile at this stranger; he smiles back. He must be in his fifties; almost bald, with a fleshy kindly face. He could be my father. Tommy and I never converse while he's eating. He's got the determination of the self-made man. Bones are sucked. His trouble is that he never relaxes. Imagine, trying to send a telegram to his foreman on a Sunday; another building his firm's demolishing. At this rate there'll be nothing left of Glasgow.

He's folding his napkin carefully. I smile as he passes and he nods. The table looks so sad, with the sprig of cherry stalks lying on the plate between the two empty chairs, like a little bit of burnt-out lightning.

I ask Tommy if he minds me going out for a cigarette. He shakes his head because his mouth's full of cherries. He'll eat my share too, then wake in the night with indigestion. I worry about his heart.

I go out on to the balcony. He's standing staring out to sea, smoke rising above his shoulder. I light up too. But I'm nervous and I spill the matches. He comes to help me pick them up. We're all fingers together; his are so soft; immaculate nails. (Tommy has half of Glasgow under his.)

"This is kind of you," I say. He has to help me up by the arm, my flapper's dress (bought, Paris) is so tight.

"Just a little accident."

"I *knew* you were Scottish," I say, using the last match to light my cigarette. (I fit mine into a holder; it's healthier. Tommy's a forty-a-day man; his fingers are filthy.)

"Which part of Scotland are you from?"

He looks anxious. "Glasgow."

"That's where I'm from too," I tell him. "North or south side? I know — you're south, like me."

But he's turned away, to look at the sea. "The colours here are amazing. It's difficult to tell where the sea stops and the sky begins."

I know why he doesn't want to talk; he's watching for the boat bringing back his wife. It won't come. He looks abandoned. But what business is this of mine? (Tommy gets on at me for worrying over stray dogs in France.)

"The tobacco here's become so harsh since the Americans took over production," he says. "My tongue's been swollen up; that's why I'm on these cigarillos."

"Take these." I hand him my packet of Craven A. Tommy's got a whole suitcase full in the bedroom. He's no respecter of customs.

"No, I'll persevere with these," he says. Then: "Did you have some of the black cherries?"

I'm taken completely by surprise. "No," I say, but I can't tell him why not. What is a twenty-five-year-old doing following a man who could be her father out of the *salle à manger* of a rather rundown Port Vendres hotel? (Tommy's calling this my Bohemian holiday.)

"I don't like cherries." What else can I say? I gave mine to Tommy so that I could follow him out.

"That's a tragedy because they're so big and juicy. I wonder if they would keep in the post" (he's looking out to sea as he says this). Then: "I've got a letter to finish. *Bonsoir.*"

When I go back in, Tommy's devoured all the cherries. It's a wonder he didn't chew the stalks too. This is the worry; a six-teen stone thirty-five-year-old man on top of you after such a meal.

After he falls asleep I go through his suitcase and find this account book. I tear out the few pages he's done calculations on. I've never done anything like this before, but I have a feeling I should keep a diary on this holiday. Tommy mustn't see it, of course.

Monday 23rd May
Wind shrieking all night, turning the net curtains into that crazy dancer we saw on top of a table — *nothing* below her white dress — at Antibes last summer. What else but an American?

24

But even this gale can't get the better of Tommy's snoring and grunting. He must be trying to push over a building.

I'm lying thinking about the mysterious Glaswegian in the corner extolling the virtues of black cherries (can cherries have *virtues*?). Maybe he's a buyer in food, looking for goodies for a Glasgow restaurant. But he doesn't look the commercial type.

I would say that he's been at this hotel for some time, the way he goes to his table. But by the time we get down to breakfast he's been, or not eating it; his napkin seems to be folded exactly as it was last night, like a little white envelope.

It's still very blowy, but I want some fresh air, and we could just bump into him. I've such a job keeping my dress from going over my head. Tommy doesn't want to walk; he'd rather sit in a café and — would you believe this? — price a demolition job for Glasgow? I'm not going to complain, though; I've got my mysterious Glaswegian (I reckon from his hands that he's a musician) to find out about.

I try to hurry Tommy down to dinner, even tying his shoelaces for him. He insists on wearing his white double-breasted suit, which means we have to find a cleaners every second day. But he won't be hurried; he says it's like bringing down a building. Rush it and accidents happen.

He isn't at his table! I'm trying to see if it's a new napkin, which means that he's gone. But if I move my chair Tommy may get suspicious. What a pity my Glaswegian isn't here, because there are black cherries again. I can have some tonight, though I'm watching the door as I pop them into my mouth. They seem bitter.

I go out to smoke on the balcony, leaving Tommy with my cheese. He's like a giant white mouse nibbling and spluttering. (God, he'd better not read this!)

I feel very lonely, standing there at the railing, staring out to sea. Has he gone in search of the occupant of the other chair? Will two of them come back to share the same stalk of black cherries? Maybe I read too many novels, but you need a bit of romance in Glasgow. I have a husband who comes home late.

Oh not tonight. Tommy making love is a demolition job.

Tuesday 24th May

Doze off and you miss the night here, it's so brief. I'm back lying in the light of an August dawn in Glasgow, waiting for Daddy to come up and kiss me before going off to the war. I'm frightened of the squeak squeak of his new boots. They must hurt.

Then I hear a crash on the stairs. Burglars! By the time I wake Tommy, they'll be miles away. Besides, he'll just say: it's not our business, as long as they haven't pinched anything from this room (especially the tenders he's pricing).

I open the door very quietly and peep out. It's him, going downstairs, laden. Now where on earth's he off to at this hour? Sneaking away because he can't afford to pay his bill?

Tommy's still snoring, but I'm getting up. Off with the negligée (another present from Tommy; transparent of course) and on with cool white cotton.

I run downstairs in my bare feet, out into the street, but there's not a sign of my mysterious Glaswegian. When Tommy comes down to breakfast (after I've smoked five cigarettes) he announces: "I'm going to hire a car and drive along the coast."

I'm aghast: "But it'll be blazing hot; we'll both get sunstroke, and you know you're too stout."

"Not if we take simple precautions."

Oh God, does that mean that he's going to buy a straw hat? It's not that I don't want to see the sea and maybe go for a swim. It's Tommy's driving: last year in a village near Cannes (name best forgotten) he ran into the local market. Strawberries went flying everywhere, down my dress, into the car. The gears were squelchy. The whole car had to be stripped down.

Fortunately there isn't a car for hire today in Port Vendres. Tommy's perspiring so much that we have to sit in the shade of a café. He soon nods off; safe enough for me to take a stroll by myself. Did I really only marry him for his money; because he swept up our crescent in an open imported American car, boasting that he had fifty men on his books? Wasn't I too young?

At dinner the mysterious Glaswegian is back at his corner table. Pea soup; Dover sole; aubergines; roast beef; followed

26

by red instead of black cherries. They look delicious, but I'm frightened to take one in case he's watching. There are some people you don't deceive.

He's certainly enjoying them, splitting them with his knife, keeping them in his mouth a long time as he looks at the empty chair. This time I go out first on to the balcony. I'm beginning to think he's gone straight up to his room, but here he is.

"How is your tongue?"

He looks surprised. "I beg your pardon?"

"Your tongue; you were having trouble with American tobacco."

He laughs. "Oh I've solved that one. I spread it in the sun to dry out the sauce they saturate it in. But I'll stay on these cigarillos just now."

Here we are chatting, when we haven't even exchanged names.

"I'm Kirsty Boyle." My hand is the first out.

"Mackintosh"; a slack grip.

Tommy comes shuffling out, white suit spattered with cherry juice.

"Mr Mackintosh is from Glasgow," I say. "This is my husband Tommy."

In a row I had with Mummy before my marriage she called Tommy an oaf; I thought it was the strain of Daddy and the war. Tommy grunts and nods as he makes for the nearest chair.

"You look pale, Tommy," I say. "Shouldn't you go and lie down?"

"You have to be very careful with the cherries; make sure they're properly washed," Mr Mackintosh tells him.

"What do you want me to do? Go through to the kitchen sink with them, then take them back to the dining-room? I pay for service, even in a dump like this," says Tommy, tapping the chair arm.

He shames me every time in public now. Some people think he's my father, and though it's a slight, I don't speak up.

"I must go and finish a letter," Mr Mackintosh says, taken aback.

"Tommy, why must you *behave* like that?"

"It was a bloody stupid thing to say about washing the cherries."

"Mr Mackintosh has been staying here for some time and knows."

"If you think this place is dirty, let's move then — *tonight*. You know I prefer bigger places. I like to be near a casino."

"No, no." I mustn't sound too hasty. "I like the atmosphere here."

Tommy falls asleep as soon as he hits the bed, which is a blessing. It's like a wall falling on one. Strange: as I write down Mr Mackintosh's words, I can hear his voice clearly, as if he's dictating.

Wednesday 25th May

I haven't shut my eyes. I've been lying, deliberately looking at the window and then at the little diamond watch Tommy gave me when he demolished a whole street in Glasgow. I'm up at six thirty, dressing very simply (white cotton for coolness; sandals). Then I sit on the bed, waiting.

I sat like that in Glasgow, until the light faded, day after day. Mummy kept saying: he'll be home any day now, you'll see; but he never came.

When I hear the click of his door I count to twenty. Then I go downstairs. He's about a hundred yards ahead of me, an easel under one arm, folding stool under the other. One leg seems to drag. I want to run up, to take the box of paints, he looks so pathetic, but that would only make it seem that I'm spying on him. So I let him get a little further ahead, but not out of sight.

We're leaving the village and it's getting very hot. My toes are on fire in the dust and I'm wishing that I'd worn shoes. In the heat-haze Mr Mackintosh seems to be shimmering as if he's about to explode, easel and stool sent flying, his straw hat spinning away.

We're walking close to the cliffs now, past the old forts. When he stops and sets down his stuff, I slip behind a rock. It's no use; I'm too close. I must give him time to get ahead, except that I could easily lose him here — and myself.

Now he's taking off his jacket and folding it carefully, before he sets up his easel. He looks much younger, in his green corduroys. He's settled on the folding stool and has a brush in his hand.

I can't see the painting from this distance, so I count up to 100. Then I begin to walk forward as casually as I can, with my hands behind my back. But I know I'm taking too big strides, as if I'm stalking something. I don't want to startle him, so I cough as I get closer. The brush stops.

"It's Mr Mackintosh, isn't it?" (God, that sounded so forced.)

He stands up. (This man is a gentleman; if Her Majesty herself came into a room Tommy would remain on his backside; he only rises to shake hands over deals.)

"Don't let me disturb you; I'm only taking a walk before breakfast." Then: "May I stay and watch?" (I'm making such a mess of this.)

"By all means."

I'm standing at his shoulder. His shirt collar's worn beneath the straw brim. I would like to touch his neck. But when I look at the brush I get a shock. What on earth's he painting?

I lean closer. Like grey jagged tombstones all piled together. I look beyond the paper on the easel. It's incredible, I would never have seen those rocks, with the sea beyond, like that. How has he managed to compress them into such a small sheet, and still show their power?

"I'm suffering from a green disease; I should have painted the big grey rock first." At least that's what I *think* he said; he was really muttering to himself.

Are these buildings in the background? But I don't want to lean any closer. It seems to me that my breathing could disturb that brush. I stand, or rather lean in silence, as if I'm not there.

Mackintosh; I'm going to have to be very careful here not to show my ignorance. I don't recall hearing that name in Glasgow. Mind you, Tommy wouldn't put a penny into paintings. (Not that he leaves walls standing to hang them on. His idea of art's the dirty magazines he buys in Paris.)

How am I going to do this?

"Mr Mackintosh —"

"Ye-s." The brush dabs.

"You're obviously a professional painter."

"I don't know what you mean by professional."

Neither do I. He must be able to feel the heat from my face. Why don't I just go instead of making a fool of myself? (That's the advantage of men like Tommy, they're easy to handle; no deep subjects.)

"It's your livelihood," I say.

"Not yet, but I'm hopeful."

Now what does that mean?

"Yesterday the wind kept blowing the easel down. Today — look."

I bend till our faces are almost touching. What I took to be part of the painting are hundreds of tiny crawling insects, all different, some with shimmering wings.

"I like to give them the chance to get out of the way of the brush." He blows gently. "Otherwise they become fossilised in the paint; that's too close to nature; a still-life Cézanne would never have approved of."

I nod; I know that name. I took Art in school. I could have made something of it, but Tommy's big American car came up the crescent. I was good at embroidery, but it couldn't be both marriage and college.

"I need good weather because I'm hoping to have an exhibition soon," Mr Mackintosh says.

"In Glasgow? Tell me when, so I can go and see it. Will they be for sale?"

He shakes his head. "Definitely not Glasgow. If it comes off it'll be in London at the Leicester Gallery. They'll all be for sale; that's what an exhibition's for. But it all depends on the weather."

Is this a hint for me to go away? Not that Tommy will wait for me for breakfast; more likely to eat mine.

"How long are you staying?" I ask.

"Indefinitely. The climate suits us — despite the none-too-gentle zephyrs."

Us? "Oh — you're here with someone." Question or statement?

"My wife. She's in London just now, having electrical treatment."

I've read about that; wires stuck to the skull; shocking pain. The poor soul; so that's why he looks so sad, with a mental wife. That's why he's got to finish the paintings, to get money for her treatment.

There are some conversations which you have to let come to a natural end. I go back to the hotel, but I don't feel like breakfast. When I tell Tommy that I've been for a walk to clear a headache, he nods, his mouth stuffed with food. He always demands bacon and eggs when he's abroad, making himself understood with sign language; an open mouth. (You should see him ordering snails.)

We sit on the balcony, but a south wind's getting up, flapping Tommy's newspaper, which irritates me. Probably his easel's been blown over. I can see him struggling with it, painting the rock (who would buy such a subject?) to pay for his mad wife's shock treatment.

He comes back about lunch-time, lugging his equipment. I go up to our room, hoping to meet him. I stand outside his door. The one opposite is open; the foot of a bed.

Rosa the patronne comes at my back.

"Cette chambre est déjà prise."

I don't understand what she means.

"La femme de ce pauvre Monsieur Mackintosh est à Londres." She clasps her heart with both hands.

At least, that's what I think she's saying, she speaks so fast. But I don't want to let her go till I find out more. She's trying to tell me how much in love they are; that's why the door's left open, so he can see her bed.

"Monsieur Mackintosh est un artiste."

"Oui, oui," she nods vigorously. "Mais (finger wagged) il est aussi un gentilhomme."

I suppose (with what one reads about Picasso) that there is a distinction.

"Madame Mackintosh – elle est –" damn it, I don't know what I want to ask, so I hold up my hand level.

"Ah, très grande, et elle a une chevelure magnifique," (shows

31

with her hands). "Comme une Comtesse."

I picture this tall beautiful woman with a weak head. It gets sadder and sadder. I'm trying to muster my appalling command of the language (Tommy thinks that everyone should speak English on the continent) but a bell goes, and the *patronne* plunges down the stairs.

Tommy is threatening to hire a car again. I suppose I must let him, because the more he hangs about the hotel, the more he eats. (The white suit's almost too tight.) Anyway, here comes that south wind again (I wet my finger and hold it up), so Mr Mackintosh is going to have a struggle with his painting.

We get a car, but the garage insists that Tommy wears goggles because of the dust. He now looks like a very large frog. He goes too fast along the coast road for me to take in anything. When he was courting me first in Glasgow, I used to think it was dare-devil, the way he overtook even trams on Great Western Road; now I think he's just dangerous.

Do I any longer, did I ever love this man? – I ask myself as the Med blurs by. I'm now beginning to dread going back to Glasgow with him.

Dinner tonight; lamb with haricots. My carnivore husband is in ecstasy, his napkin tucked into his neck, his plate heaped with slices of meat. Mr Mackintosh seems to be enjoying his also, but he eats as he paints; slow, studied.

I go out for a smoke before I get drenched in gravy. The sky is clouding over; I really should go up for a cardigan.

Me: "Did you make any progress with the Rock today?"

Mr M: (lighting his cigarillo) "It got windy about midday, but I'm fairly pleased with the morning's work. I went for a walk up to the Fort this afternoon; the genista's wonderful."

Me: "Genista?"

Mr M: "Broom. It seems to have appeared suddenly, as if by magic; so yellow, such scent. I'll have to tell my wife about it in the letter; it's a great pity she's missing it."

Me: "Have you any news of how she's getting on in London?"

Mr M: (sadly) "No letter today; probably tomorrow. But I think the electrical treatment's working."

But how can she write him sensible letters if that's what

she's getting? Poor soul; he writes, telling her everything that's going on (including the inquisitive Glasgow woman with the gluttonous husband) but she can't take in a word because of the volts.

Me: "It's wonderful what they can do nowadays."

Mr M: "She would never complain; I hope it's not painful."

Me: (not convincing) "I shouldn't think so."

Mr M: "It's supposed to stimulate the heart."

So that's what the *patronne* meant when she clutched her left breast! Not love (that's inherent), but a weak heart being treated. That means I can go on talking to him, without being frightened of saying (*asking*) the wrong thing.

But he obviously senses this because he puts out his smoke and says he's got to go and finish his letter "to my wife. It turns into a kind of a chronicle; a bit of writing, a bit of painting and so on. Incidentally, how *do* you spell chronicle?"

I think I get it right.

Mr M: "That's a pity; I've been spelling it with a y instead of an i."

Me: "What does it matter, as long as your wife understands?"

Tommy's drunk far too much tonight. He seems to get heavier every day. This bed is going to give soon. I mustn't let him drive Mr Mackintosh's words (he said a lot today) out of my head before I can get them down in my chronicle. Why do I feel they're so important?

Thursday 26th May

I wake in the dawn, but it's dull, drizzling; no sound of the artist afoot. Mr Mackintosh is in the dining-room. There are only the three of us, and Tommy is dumb and droopy with a hangover.

The maid is explaining something to Mr Mackintosh. I listen very hard, trying to keep up. Today's Ascension? Un fête? Mr Mackintosh looks very glum.

Mr M: "Pas de courrier?"

The maid shrugs.

Because it's not walking weather we go into the lounge.

Mr Mackintosh is reading the *News of the World*, with the *Despatch* on the table. This pleases Tommy no end. He offers Mr Mackintosh a Craven A in exchange for a read at the *Despatch*.

"Help yourself," says Mr Mackintosh, but refuses the cigarette.

Tommy spends the morning in the stock exchange page, which means that I can't speak to Mr Mackintosh. It's maddening. I try to will Tommy to fall asleep, but when it comes to money he's wide-awake. Ask him to read a book, though. . . .

Mr Mackintosh goes out and I don't see him till dinner. Just as I'm about to follow him out Tommy says: "I want to go to a casino tonight."

"We're not going near one," I tell him angrily. "The last time you lost thousands of francs."

"That's French money."

"It doesn't matter; it's still too much when you convert it into our money."

"But the business is doing well," he says. "And there's another big contract coming up which somebody in the Corporation told me I would get."

"Go tonight and that's us finished," I warn him. But people at the other tables are beginning to look at us, so I hurry out.

Too late; Mr Mackintosh has had his smoke and gone upstairs. I pick the warm stump of the cigarillo from the ashtray. Damn Tommy; if he puts a hand near me tonight — why am I writing down what *he* says?

Friday 27th May
A glorious dawn; not a breath of wind. I hear him go out at seven, but I've been up, dressed, for a good hour, looking at Tommy lying there, with his loud mouth even when he's sleeping. Mummy was right; a great mistake. I should have done something useful with my life.

Since I know where he's going there's no need to follow him so fast. By the time I arrive he's painting.

Me: "The Rock will soon be finished."

Mr M: "God willing, if I get a few more days of this weather."

I stand behind him, making sure I don't cast a shadow.

Me: "If you'll have your show in Glasgow instead of London I'll bring all my friends to buy your paintings."

The brush hesitates.

Mr M: "I'll never show a picture in Glasgow. I doubt if I'll ever set foot in the place again."

Something very bad obviously happened to him in Glasgow: but how to put it without prying?

Me: "That's very sad, when it's your home city."

Mr M: "It never showed me much —"

Let a few seconds pass; hold your breath.

Mr M: "I'm quite pleased with the way this is shaping."

I can't ask him about Glasgow again.

Me: "Will you teach me to paint?"

It's not an impulsive question. I've been thinking about it for most of the night. It's a way of going back; that's what Daddy would have wanted. I'll make Tommy stay out here for a few more weeks, or else leave me here. Then? Back to Glasgow, to college.

Mr M: "I can't teach anyone to paint because I'm still learning myself."

Me: "I could pay you for lessons."

Mr M: (shaking his head) "It wouldn't be fair on either of us."

The conversation appears to have come to a halt. I'd better leave now, before I spoil his painting. But I'm close to tears as I go back through the hot dawn, carrying a sandal in each hand. I suppose I've always been used to having my own way. But I really would love to work with him, sitting beside him, with my arms and feet bare in the sun while he leans over, touching my drawing with his gentle hand, showing me where I've gone wrong.

I sit on the balcony of the hotel, dozing off because I've been getting up so early. I'm back in Glasgow, waiting for my father to return (he volunteered for the Commercial Company). Every time I hear the letter-box —

Someone's shouting. I dash into the hall, thinking that

Tommy's dropped dead! Mr Mackintosh is standing there, laden with his painting equipment. The *patronne's* pointing with three fingers up the stairs, shouting: "Voilà sur le lit!"

Is it a mouse? He puts down his things in a heap and hurries upstairs, pursued by the patronne, still shouting. She emerges, clasping her hands.

"Une lettre! Une lettre de la Comtesse!"

I'm half-way up the stairs. Suddenly I feel jealous, thinking of him sitting up there, devouring her letter. Tommy has never sent me one in his life; not even a card. He saves his calligraphy for a scrawl on demolition contracts.

After lunch I go back out on to the balcony. It's a bit overcast, but still warm. At about four I see Mr Mackintosh going out for a walk. I feel like running after him. Then I do something I'm ashamed to put down on paper. I go out into the hall, making sure the *patronne's* not about before I tiptoe upstairs.

The door of Mrs Mackintosh's room is still open. It's very neat, all the clothes put away, nothing on the dressing-table. I expect she's taken her toilet stuff to London with her. I would like to look at her clothes but I'm afraid the wardrobe will squeak. The room seems rather cold.

There's a photograph of two people on the wall. I have to kneel on the bed to see it. It's him, younger. How handsome he is; dark hair, stylish swept-up moustache (almost like some of the *gigolos* we saw in Italy several summers ago; Tommy had another word for them) and his tie a huge floppy bow. He looks so free, at ease, not like he is now.

She's standing close to him, between them a kind of panel (a painting waiting to be hung?) of tall figures and what looks like foliage I'm certain I've seen somewhere before. The way it flows, it's very different from the Rock.

She's taller than he is; beautiful; auburn-looking hair. I love her dress. (She must be an artist herself, maybe an embroiderer.) I could stay for hours on my knees, looking at them, but I'm terrified the *patronne* will come up. The way she talks, this room is a shrine.

It's so tempting to open a drawer and find out who he is,

once and for all, because they both look *distinguished* people. (I certainly don't mean socially; not that you could take Tommy anywhere in Glasgow.) But I daren't touch anything in here.

At dinner I compare him with the photograph above our heads. He's still a good-looking man, though more reserved in the way he dresses. He has this peculiar habit I haven't mentioned before. He gets a full bottle of wine with every meal, and drinks it down to exactly half, which he leaves. The next meal it's a full bottle again. Surely the *patronne*'s not charging him for a full bottle each time? (Tommy can drink down two bottles at each meal, and drain my glass. He's also got whisky upstairs. I think he's getting heavy on it.)

Cherries (red) again tonight. But he doesn't touch them! He's rising, nodding as he goes out. I give him five minutes.

Me: "Are you all right?"

Mr M: "You're lucky, not eating these cherries. They've been overripe; I've had an upset stomach for a few days."

(Tommy's been stuffing them; it's a wonder his gut's not fermenting with all that drink and food.)

Me: "Does that mean work on the Rock has stopped?"

Mr M: "No, I've managed to keep going; I must get it finished for the exhibition."

Me: "Will you stay here all summer?"

Mr M: "No; once my wife gets back, we'll go up to Mont Louis when it starts to get really hot. We do that every summer."

Me: (surprised) "How long have you been out here?"

Mr M: "Let me see — since 1923."

Me: "Lucky *you*."

Mr M: (going quiet again) "I wouldn't say that. It's getting chilly, isn't it? I hope this doesn't mean a change."

Me: "We'll both pray hard for sunshine so that the Rock can be finished."

Mr M: "If I got the whole of tomorrow —"

But here comes Tommy. Well if he thinks I'm going to the cleaners again tomorrow he's mistaken.

Tommy: "These cherries are terrific; I don't know why you won't take them."

He's going to embarrass me in front of Mr Mackintosh, telling him how I eat cherries in Glasgow.

Mr M: "They've certainly upset me."

"And you're the one who went on and on about washing them," Tommy says, shaking his head. "You're havering, Mister; I've been eating them every night and there's nothing wrong with me."

At that moment I wish that Tommy was standing under one of his own buildings. Why do I come to the continent with such a savage?

I make my resolution as I lie in bed, having persuaded Tommy to have another nightcap of Johnnie Walker instead of his conjugal rights (such rights are usually one-sided, weighted in favour of the man). Since Mr Mackintosh won't teach me to paint, I'll sell the diamond watch in Port Vendres and buy the Rock from him. Obviously he won't part with it before the exhibition, but he can put my name on the back and have it sent to Glasgow to me. By then I hope to be independent of Tommy.

Saturday 28th May

A lovely morning; he goes out at 6.30. I must give him an hour. But he's not there! I *can't* have come to the wrong place; there's the Rock, the buildings behind it. Did he take ill on the way? But I would have met him.

Of course I didn't see him leave the hotel. He may have taken all his things and gone because he thinks I've been pestering him. I sit down on a fallen tree, my fists clenched. I really felt I was making a friend, somebody I could talk to. Tommy's diamond watch flares on my wrist; I feel like taking it off and throwing it as far as I can.

I make my way slowly back to the hotel, dragging my sandals through the dust. I'll stop in a café for a drink, then go and tell Tommy that I can't stand it any more. I want more for my life than money from ruined buildings.

I can't stay here, because that will mean taking money from Tommy. No; I'll go back to Glasgow alone and get a job, so that I can get money for college. I really want to better myself.

There are things Mr Mackintosh says about art. If I don't understand them at the time, how can I write them later in my chronicle?

But Tommy isn't in the hotel. He'll be away at the post office, sending another of his telegrams to his foreman. We're booked in here for another week; I want to go this afternoon. I can stay with Mummy for a while.

Who do I see from the balcony walking along the street? I don't care; I rush out to meet Mr Mackintosh. I could hug him.

Me: "I went to the Rock but you weren't there. I've been so worried that you'd been taken ill somewhere because of the cherries."

Mr M: "That's very considerate of you" (he means it). "But I went to draw the Fort instead. I have to keep several works going at the one time if I'm to have forty paintings for my Leicester Gallery exhibition."

He's put his drawing folder down on the reception desk. CRM is painted in stylish black letters. This is my chance, at last. I take a deep breath.

Me: (touching the folder) "What does CRM stand for?"

Mr M: "It was a lovely morning."

I have to risk it, because I know that this is the last opportunity I'll have, so I repeat myself.

Mr M: (with great reluctance) "Charles Rennie Mackintosh."

I try not to show in my face that I'm no wiser. But I can't offend him by dropping it, so I have to think quickly because he's now got his drawing folder under his arm, his foot on the bottom step.

Me: "I think I've seen some of your paintings in Glasgow."

Mr M: "Really? You couldn't have seen them in a gallery; it must have been in a private house. A few of my friends have one or two. We must have mutual friends."

I want to change the subject, but he's watching me closely.

Me: "I just don't know; but your name means something to me. It's going to niggle at me all day."

He hesitates, his hand on the banister.

Mr M: "I wasn't a full-time painter in Glasgow. I was an architect."

This is getting out of hand; he must be able to feel the heat from my face.

Me: "That's what it is; I've seen your name on a building."

Mr M: "But my name isn't on anything I built in Glasgow; not that I built very much."

Me: "Name some of them, then I'll know."

Mr M: (reluctantly) "Well, there's the Art School, and Miss Cranston's tearooms —"

I know it now! I'm a wee girl again. Daddy doesn't work on Saturday afternoon. I fetch the horn so that he can put on his brightest boots. He's getting his watch-chain looped across his waistcoat. Half-way up Sauchiehall Street I begin to girn, and he has to carry me.

It's always the same ritual. Up the strange stairs in his arms; through the glass doors that look like broken bits of mirror stuck together. He sits me down on the high-backed silver chair.

Here's the game. I have to peep round the chair, staring at the big panel on the wall. Daddy says that as soon as I see the fairy queen stepping from the panel, I've to wish for something nice.

When I turn round, there's a big creamy cake on my plate, and a funny-looking spoon to eat it with. I always get cream on my chin, but Daddy wipes it with the handkerchief from his breast pocket.

That's the panel that's between Mr and Mrs Mackintosh in her bedroom upstairs. I would like to tell him that his Room de luxe in the Willow Tearoom, Miss Cranston's, was a magic grotto to a wee girl; but Daddy didn't come back from France, and I've never set foot since in the Willow. (Is it still there?)

Me: "I think I'll go and lie down; the sun's given me a headache."

I slept through dinner. When Tommy came up, drunk, I pretended to be still sleeping. He soon gave up.

Sunday 29th May

I am down early to breakfast, but Mr Mackintosh is already there. Is he going queer? He sweeps his hand slowly over his wife's chair, as if trying to summon up her spirit. Then he holds his hand up against the glare of the window-pane. There is a membrane of a cobweb between his spread fingers.

When he passes my table he asks: "Are you feeling better this morning?"

I'm confused.

Mr M: "Your headache?"

Me: "Oh, that's gone; I had a sound sleep. And you: will the Rock be finished today?"

He shakes his head. "I never work on a Sunday."

He obviously sees my disappointment because he says: "I'm going for a walk; would you like to come?"

We are walking in a cool shaded place of trees and flowers, perfume in the air.

Mr M: "We call this Happy Valley; my wife and I often come here."

Me: "Will she be coming back soon?"

Mr M: "A few more weeks; I'll take the train to Perpignan to meet her."

Me: "You'll have done more paintings by then?"

Mr M: (laughing) "If I don't she'll think I've been lying in my letters. I write every day, but may not post it for several days. I have to watch the weight, for the cost."

I stumble where stone is exposed. He has my arm.

Me: "Why did you give up being an architect in Glasgow?" (I could add: there must be plenty of opportunity, the number of buildings my husband's knocking down.)

Mr M: "It didn't work out, for various reasons; I don't like talking about it. When the past goes wrong, you have to try and put it behind you."

Just like me with Tommy.

Mr M: "Anyway, I'm a painter now, or trying to be. Paper's easier to work with than stone. You don't need to get planning approval, and you can tear it up if you aren't satisfied."

Me: "Does your wife paint?"

Mr M: "No, but she believes in me; that's the great thing."

Me: "Does your wife —"

41

Mr M: "I think we'd better turn now, before we get sunstroke. Look at that."

He pulls out the pocket of his green corduroy trousers, to show me the hole.

Mr M: "I've probably lost money through that."

Me: "I'll sew it after dinner;" I've got a little kit in my room, and a husband who's always tearing things.

Mr M: "Thank you; but I'll ask the *patronne*."

Me: "She thinks the world of you — and Mrs Mackintosh."

Mr M: "We've been there a long time, summer and winter. I suppose it's our home now. In fact" (he stops) "I would like my ashes scattered here."

There are a lot of smart motor-cars parked outside the hotel, and the dining-room is quite full. Two little children have been put at Mr Mackintosh's table. (The parents are at the next one, with even more children.)

They look angelic, sitting either side of him, the little girl in Mrs Mackintosh's chair. But then they start kicking at each other under the table, and poor Mr Mackintosh's shins get in the way. Still, he smiles through it all.

I am on the balcony with my cigarette after lunch.

Mr M: "There's a sailing ship in the harbour, crammed full of wine."

Me: "Perhaps we should stow away on it."

Mr M: "No; I think I've done enough moving about. Anyway I only like wine in moderation."

Tommy comes in behind us, searching for Sunday papers. He drank a bottle with his lunch.

Me: "Tommy, Mr Mackintosh is an architect. He built the Glasgow Art School."

Tommy: "That's the place above Sauchiehall Street."

Mr Mackintosh nods, pleased.

Tommy is sucking his Craven A alight. Then: "It would be a difficult demolition job because of all that glass."

Mr Mackintosh is no longer there. I slap Tommy; then I run upstairs. But the *patronne* is standing outside his door, waving her arms.

"*Non, non, il écrit*" (she scribbles on her palm) "*à la Comtesse.*"

Monday 30th May

I have had a dream; my father with bloody face, his uniform in tatters, staggering out of the Mackintosh mural in the Room de luxe.

I listen for Mr Mackintosh going. He's probably slipped out early, quietly, after Tommy's insult. I've decided; as soon as the shops open I'm going to sell the diamond watch, and go and find Mr Mackintosh. I want the strength of the Rock on my wall in whatever future I have.

But it's a grey morning, with mist swirling in. There will be no work done on the Rock today, by the looks of it; but I'm still determined to buy it in advance.

Mr Mackintosh is at breakfast. He nods to me. He doesn't look angry about Tommy's insult. (I shall explain to him later what I'm married to.)

The *patronne* comes in and puts a telegram on Tommy's napkin. I look at it upside down and see the Glasgow postmark. We've still got another week here, and I want longer. I'll make him buy me a paintbox today.

I would tear up that envelope on his plate, except that the *patronne* (obviously a gossip) will tell him about it. Mr Mackintosh is now breaking bread in his fists.

Tommy opens the envelope with a filthy finger. Then he rises again.

"Got to get moving," he says.

I turn the telegram round.

SERIOUS TROUBLE OVER FINNIESTON
CONTRACT stop Macleod foreman

Me: (vehemently) "I'm not having my holiday interrupted by that. You can go."

Tommy stands over me, his big gut pressing against my arm.

"This is about money; you can't stay."

I look for Mr Mackintosh but he's left the hotel. As I pack, crying, the fog lifts like a curtain. There are three huge grey battleships outside the harbour. I must put this book into my luggage.

Postscript

Charles Rennie Mackintosh died in London in 1928, from a cancer that had started in his tongue.

The Rock is now the property of a private collector in England.

ALEX HAMILTON

Car Sticker

George Brownlee was 38, rich and athletic.

Sam Rogers was 38.

George Brownlee lived in a bachelor penthouse in Newton Mearns, owned and directed a city centre advertising consultancy, and drove a mint-condition '64 Chevrolet.

Sam Rogers walked to his counter in the local Social Security office.

George Brownlee kept a couple of pounds worth of 10p pieces in his glove compartment, and carried a fountain pen, two cheque books and a deck of credit cards.

Sam Rogers' waking hours were harassed by an ever-burgeoning mound of unanswerable letters from two bank managers, a building society, a personal loan broker and three finance companies.

George Brownlee used cash for feeding parking meters.

Sam Rogers' wife had gone to work complaining and reluctant.

George Brownlee's *forte* was presentation.

Sam Rogers' wife had given up ironing his shirts and pressing his trousers.

George Brownlee was immaculate.

Sam Rogers was a lost cause.

Annie Henderson had married when she was 23, become a full-time housewife and expectant mother at 24, and returned to employment in her 37th year.

Sam Rogers' only child had miscarried in its mother's womb at the age of 3 months, and had never had a sibling.

George Brownlee's personal secretary had left him to have a baby the week after Sam Rogers had been invited to visit one of his bank managers.

Annie Rogers' counsellor at the Department of Employment sub-office had sent her to be interviewed by the owner-director of a city centre advertising consultancy.

Sam Rogers' wife was picked up by her boss at 08.50 every weekday, and given a lift to work in a mint-condition '64 Chevrolet.

George Brownlee was at business most weekends.

Sam Rogers gave his counter no thought between Friday 17.00 and Monday 08.30.

Annie Rogers' services were necessary to her boss whenever he was working.

George Brownlee was passionate about his job.

Sam Rogers got into the habit of shopping on Saturdays and hoovering on Sundays.

Annie Rogers no longer complained about having to earn.

George Brownlee was synonymous with the company called after him and registered under his name.

CAR STICKER

Sam Rogers paid an inordinate proportion of his salary to the Inland Revenue.

Annie Rogers had a cup of coffee with the Brownlee and Co accountant while they waited for the boss to come out of a meeting.

George Brownlee paid almost no income tax.

Sam Rogers' wife persuaded him to take out a £60,000 Joint Life–First Death insurance policy on their marriage.

Annie Rogers had to service her employer at a weekend presentation he was making to potential clients in an Aviemore hotel.

George Brownlee and his secretary left for the mountains at 16.30 on the Friday.

Sam Rogers' salary advice indicated a significant raising of his tax coding.

Annie Rogers enjoyed the ride in the Chevrolet, the ride in the cable car, the ride on the ski slopes.

George Brownlee felt easy about the weekend after the drive, the fresh air, the exercise.

Sam Rogers signed a hire purchase agreement on his Saturday shopping expedition, and used his new income tax relief as deposit on an American circuit in the Scalextrix model motor car series.

Annie Rogers worked hard in her boss's interests.

George Brownlee worked hard on his prospective clients.

Sam Rogers worked hard at his track layout.

Annie Rogers telephoned her husband on the Sunday to say she would be home at about 21.30.

George Brownlee asked the porter to check the Chevrolet's water and oil levels, and make sure its tyre pressures were *comme il faut*.

Sam Rogers tested his resprayed '64 Chevrolet on the gradient which snaked up the papier-mâché bridge and over his bathtub.

Annie Rogers glanced at the dash-mounted clock, and estimated that she would be home in ten minutes.

George Brownlee clicked on the radio for a time-check, and pressed hard on the accelerator as they came on to the Kingston Bridge.

Sam Rogers removed his watch in case it got wet, and placed it carefully on the touring map which he had used to calculate the distance from Aviemore to the Clyde.

Annie Rogers noticed something glistening on the Bridge at the beginning of the stretch which was highest above the water.

George Brownlee eased off his right foot and went into a swerve.

Sam Rogers revved hard on his control panel.

Annie Rogers mangled her rib cage and blinded her right eye as she went through the windscreen.

George Brownlee wept silently as the radio announcer informed him that it was 21.15.

Sam Rogers smiled as the '64 Chevrolet hit his broken milk bottle, splintered his matchstick guardrail and splatted into his bathwater.

CAR·STICKER

Sam Rogers had not heard from his wife by 20.30, so he destroyed his weekend's work.

Sam Rogers had heard from the police by 21.30.

Sam Rogers had identified his wife's body by 00.30.

Sam Rogers had drunk half a bottle of gin by 04.30.

Sam Rogers had telephoned his insurance company by 11.30.

DILYS ROSE

Child's Play

I'm learning my lesson. I'm not even supposed to be playing with you, Arabella, so sit up like a good girl or I'll have to put you to bed and you'll be in disgrace. That's what I'm in. I know it's dark Arabella. I'm not allowed the light on because that's not disgrace. Being in the dark's disgrace. Doing nothing's disgrace. If anybody comes I'll have to hide you under the covers.

You'd cry if you were a crying doll but you don't have the bit inside for crying. Sonya, that's Wendy's doll, cries real tears if you put water in her mouth. She's got a key in her back for the noise. Sonya wets her pants as well. It's the same water. She cries and wets at the same time. That's what Jenny did today, before the lump stuck and the car came and she went away with the fairies. People have a lump in the throat for crying. It grows until the water comes out of your eyes unless you can hold it in. Holding it in is brave but Jenny held it in too long. You've got to swallow it.

I wanted a doll like Sonya but she was too dear so I got you. Wendy's richer. I'm not poor but I'm not rich, I'm comfortable. That's because of sacrifices. Poor people don't know about sacrifices. Jenny Pilly's poor. She's here today and gone tomorrow.

Jenny's mum's a fly-by-night.

She does the moonlight flit. She doesn't like the scheme so she runs away when it's dark and goes gallivanting. The scheme's at the end of our street but our street's not the scheme. That starts after the witch's house. The witch flies by night as well but she

50

doesn't really fly, she sits on her broom. Running up the witch's path and ringing her doorbell is brave. If she catches you, you turn into a dead bird on her fireplace.

I'm not allowed on the scheme. The houses only have numbers, not names as well. Our house is detached. That means it's got a gate and a hedge with a garden right round the house, and it's got two doors and it's alone. If a house has a Siamese twin it's a semi. My mum doesn't like semis or houses with numbers.

I don't want to rub shoulders with Tom, Dick and Harry.

My mum says that. I've never seen people rubbing shoulders. Cows do it sometimes when they're being itchy but people can scratch themselves.

Are you listening Arabella? I'm going to be strict with you for your own good. You'll thank me when you're older. I'm learning my lesson so you've got to learn yours. I've got the slipper right here, my girl. I'm keeping my eye on you. I don't like it Arabella, it hurts me more than you. Now give Mummy a kiss, or I'll give you away to the tinks.

Wendy's been my best friend for a whole week. Wendy hates Jenny Pilly so I have to hate her as well.

Jenny Pilly's not just silly
she's a guttersnipe,
she's got nits and chappy lips
and all she gets to eat is tripe.

Wendy sang her song in the playground, and Jenny's face turned red and she said a swear-word. Wendy sang the song again louder and this time Jenny grabbed Wendy's jotter and wrote TITS on it with a red pencil. The teacher's the only one who's allowed to use a red pencil. Wendy was nearly crying, she had the lump in her throat but not the water in her eyes. Dunkie Begg got the strap for scribbling BUMS on his jotter. TITS is the same as BUMS, it's dirty. So is PISS and FANNY's worse than dirty, it's disgusting. You get a hundred lines just for saying FANNY so don't ever let me hear you saying that word Arabella, if you do learn to talk.

Look at you. What a tyke you are. You're as bad as Jenny. I'll have to send you away to live on the scheme if this goes on, or I'll give you away to the tinks, wait and see. A tink will turn you into brass or she'll take you everywhere in the rag-bag or she'll give you to her baby with the runny nose. She doesn't even have a house on the scheme, you know. She's not got a penny to her name, just bits of gold in her teeth.

Tinks are tykes and guttersnipes are common hussies. Hussies are a sort of lady, like starlings are a sort of bird. Hussies paint their toe-nails and paint the town red. When Jenny's mum paints the town red, Jenny gets to stay up really late. My mum has a special voice for hussies, a faraway voice and she looks over the hussy's shoulder when she makes the voice. The lady in the chemist's shop with the white lipstick is a hussy. When my mum buys the toothpaste and the lady wraps it up for her, she says thank you to the shelf.

Don't roll your eyes like that, Arabella. If the wind changes your eyes will stick that way — you'll be cross-eyed and see everything back to front. Jenny could only see stars until the man brought the gas mask. That wasn't supposed to be the consequence but now she can stay off school. Jenny's not good at anything at school. She's nearly always bottom. If I'm not top or nearly top I'm in disgrace but when Jenny was bottom in spelling *her* mum gave her sweets. Sweets are better than a rose from the inkblock. You get the rose for five gold stars but you can't do anything with the rose. I told my mum about the sweets for being bottom and she said that's the kind of thing riff-raff do. She said it in the voice she has for hussies. Birds of a feather flock together, my dad said. That's a saying. It means people are like birds, there's different kinds, like doves and starlings. With people it's riff-raff which are never-never and common which are undesirable. Poor ones have faces like marbles and rich ones are rough diamonds. You'll be clever like me if you learn all the words.

Jenny lives in a flat on the never-never. Her name's in a book. We got a story one time about never-never land where nobody ever grew up but that's not the scheme. There's lots of old people on the scheme and you've got to grow up to be old. Jenny's never-never is having your name in a book. A man comes to your house with the book and a suitcase. Sometimes he has a dog with him that's nearly a wolf. You've got to give him money. The Clean-Easy man comes to our house and the Onion Johnny but not the man with the suitcase. He doesn't go to Wendy's house either, the tick man.

My mum likes me to play with Wendy. She's the lesser of two evils. Her dad's a rough diamond. So is Mr de Rollo next door. He's got lots of shiny things in his house that sparkle and a silver car which lights up in the dark, like the stars. He's a dark horse as well. He's got black hair. Mrs de Rollo's young and has shiny blonde hair out of a bottle. Mr de Rollo made himself by climbing out of the gutter. Rough diamonds are very rich because diamonds are very dear. Mr de Rollo's got liquid gold in a bottle. My dad likes Mr de Rollo's liquid gold but the man's got no breeding.

Breeding is what birds do once they've got a nest.
Breeding is how you tell the sheep from the goats.

I told you Arabella, you'll be cross-eyed. You'll see everything wrong, like the magic mirrors at the shows. One blows you up fat like a balloon and one makes you long and thin like a clothes-pole and one makes you turn wavy. It's not like the witch's magic. If they had a mirror that turned you rich if you were poor, that would be real magic. But if you were rich to begin with, you'd turn poor. Jenny would turn into Wendy and Wendy would turn into Jenny. I'd have to turn into somebody but I couldn't turn rich or poor from comfortable. I'd be like the wavy mirror. Jenny could be my best friend instead of Wendy.

If Jenny was my best friend, maybe I wouldn't have to write thank-you letters. She never has to. I have to write if I get a present, always, even if it's horrible I have to write and say it's lovely.

My mum says I mustn't look a gift horse in the mouth.

Auntie Eunice is a gift horse but I never see her, she just sends the presents so I can't look her in the mouth. Real horses are nice but they've got huge teeth. Auntie Eunice must have huge teeth too. One time I asked my mum if I could get a present on the never-never, so I could send it back if I didn't like it. She said the day that happens it will be over her dead body. She says that about me staying up to watch the grown-up programmes. Jenny's allowed to watch them but I'm not because they're tripe and tripe is common. There's lots of kissing and crying but the kissing is unsuitable. On the television people kiss on the lips, like this . . . they go on for ages and it's truelove.

Truelove is unsuitable.

The kissing I do isn't truelove because I don't get a kiss. It's called a thank-you kiss or an I'm sorry kiss and it's really only a half kiss because somebody turns their face to the side and I've got to do it to their cheek. Cheek-by-jowl. It's the same when I'm in disgrace, my mum won't kiss back.

They don't have disgrace at Sunday School, just at real school and at home. You don't have to be quiet or good at tests and have breeding. You just have to give all your clothes away to the tinks and the Loving Shepherd will save you, even if you're bad. That's because of magic. They've got that mirror, Arabella, they've got one very far away. It's in the Kingdom of Heaven where you never die. But you have to be dead to get there, I think. You can even give away your new clothes and it's not ungrateful. I can give away all the presents from Auntie Eunice. You see, the poor inherit the earth. They get the world when the rich people die. The rich people turn poor and go to the Kingdom of Heaven and the poor inherit the world. The world becomes Heaven on Earth. That's the magic and nobody has to live on the scheme anymore.

It's because of magic I'm in disgrace. You see, there's different kinds of magic, there's flying on a broom and magic mirrors and there's the kind Wendy does to people if they don't do the dare. It's called "you are getting sleepy" and I was holding Jenny's arms behind her back so Wendy could do the magic with her fingers. Wendy must have done too much of the trick because you're not supposed to see stars and hit your head. You're just supposed to fall asleep and wake up in Wendy's spell. Jenny didn't wake up at all. Not even when the Jani did the kiss of life, not even when they put the gas mask on her face. Jenny's in the dark now, like me, but she's not in disgrace. She can't see even with her eyes open.

I've got to learn my lesson.

The Kingdom of Heaven is over my dead body.

Rough diamonds thank their lucky stars.

Element is tyke. Guttersnipe is undesirable.

Birds of a feather are elements.

Fly-by-nights are dark horses.

Spare the rod and spoil the consequences.

Breeding makes you comfortable.

Riff-raff flock together.

Cheek-by-jowls rub shoulders.

Gallivanters paint the town red.

Never-never land is down the drain.

Have you got that, Arabella?

VALERIE THORNTON

Crane Diver

No one had ever believed him, that one summer evening he had wandered on to the docks, under the legs of the biggest crane, and climbed the steel ladder, up, up, and up into the swaying heights of the counterweights and control house.

The view over the city had been inspiring — the smoking derelict docklands, with miles of kingfisher-walled warehouses; the sun-tinted towers of distant churches; the cars, like insects, creeping one after the other along the expressway. Clinging to the drifting girders, he felt like the most successful man in the world.

He crawled, monkey-fashion, along the steel lacework of the jib until he crouched, hundreds of feet up, above the wrinkling khaki river. A flock of sunstruck pigeons whirled in harmony around the control house roof.

It was so perfect that he knew he could do it. He stood up, balancing against the breeze, feeling on top of the world. Slowly he raised his hands above his head, cast a glance upwards into the icy sky, then, just before he lost his balance, he chose to rise on tiptoe and launch himself into a taut dive. He tipped off the jib and began to tilt through the sunset.

The sound which came from him was an involuntary shriek of pure joy — he cared neither if he lived nor if he died. His body, pointed like a shuttle, wove a slow circle through the air, hurtling ever downwards to the peaky grey surface. By chance, his dive had him angled perfectly to enter the water with a splashless "glup" at some dangerously high velocity.

The shock of the water stopping his flight, and of the vicious cold, prevented him from realising immediately that he was still alive. His clothing dragged in the dark water and he started to fight his way upward to the dull light above. Disbelieving and stunned, he gasped as he broke the surface, returning to an almost unchanged peachy evening.

The impetus of his dive still with him, he floundered in his shoes and jacket to the nearest quayside ladder and clambered up the vertical green wall. Once on the quay, he squeezed the edges of his jacket and emptied his shoes. He looked up to the monstrous structure towering above him and scarcely believed that he'd actually dived from yon threadlike piece of lattice-work. Yet he was certainly soaking and he remembered the exhilaration of his descent. He looked around to see if there had been any witnesses to his dive. The docks remained silent and deserted as rust-coloured sunlight flooded the area.

Consequently, when he told anyone he'd dived off the biggest of the dockland cranes into the Clyde, and just for fun, no one believed him.

So, tonight, he'd told them to come and watch him do it again.

But this time he was afraid. The metal seemed hostile as he hand-over-handed his way up. The evening was still and thundery. He had to get it over. Below, the river lay like sheet steel.

The angle of the jib was changed, but he crawled automatically along the arm until he reached the end. He could barely make out their pinpoint pale faces, upturned. He just wanted to get it over. Careless, he repeated the movements of the first time, toppling headfirst towards the grey below. He felt no inclination to make a sound, not even when he realised there was no reflection expanding to meet him.

His last thought was, "They'll still never believe me, dammit."

Two weeks later, a fifteen-foot fence with angled rows of barbed wire at the top prevented further unauthorised access to the crane.

FREDERIC LINDSAY

Die Laughing

Is this funny?

AMERICAN: You'll have heard, sir, of our trouble with the garbage scow out of New York?

PROVOST: Eh . . . na.

AMERICAN: No one would take her. You see what I'm saying?

PROVOST: Ye want us tae take her.

AMERICAN: Not *that* one, no. But we have . . . what we call "human factor loads". And the thing we're interested in offering you is our investment in a human factor load disposal facility. Here in beautiful Dunburgh.

JANITOR: That sounds tae me like a load o shite.

PROVOST: Haud yer tongue!

AMERICAN: Does he have to be here?

PROVOST: A wee bit bother wi the heating. He'll no be a minute. (Whispers) The wife's brother — you understand. (Aloud) Now, where were we, a load of — no, of course not — what exactly?

AMERICAN: We prefer the term human factor load.

PROVOST: Prefer . . .?

JANITOR: Ye mean it *is* shite? Get out of here!

PROVOST: Ooh — ooh — dinna be hasty.

JANITOR: American shite!

AMERICAN: No Blacks or Hispanics! Could guarantee that.

PROVOST: Oh, I don't think we would concern ourselves wi what colour it was. Not in Dunburgh. To be honest wi ye, I take a wee bit o pride in that.

AMERICAN: A proud people, sir. Of course. In fact — don't mistake me; I'm no liberal — but the stuff would be pretty much all the one colour. Could guarantee that.

PROVOST: As ye can see, there are things we take a firm line on. I hope ye won't take that the wrong way. Good, good. Now about jobs — did ye have any particular number in mind?

AMERICAN: It would depend on the unit consumption factor.

JANITOR: Ye mean ye want us tae eat it?

PROVOST: Will you be quiet! Of course, he doesn't . . . want us . . . want us to . . . (Trails off as the AMERICAN nods seriously)

AMERICAN: Interdependence. That's where the world's at for tomorrow.

JANITOR: You shit and we eat it.

AMERICAN: Only the product of good middle-class neigh-bourhoods. A lot of them would be vegetarians — could almost guarantee that.

PROVOST: These last three years there's been an awful amount of unemployment about the place. That's the truth of it.

AMERICAN: You'd be in on the ground floor. Get a jump on the competition. New technology. Get out there and sell what you've got to offer. You'd open up new markets.

JANITOR: Right enough. We've had links like that wi England for years.

AMERICAN: Think positively. Didn't you people start the industrial revolution? You could be shipping the stuff in from all over Europe.

Henri Bergson (1859-1941) held to the opinion that what makes us laugh is the sight of living creatures behaving as if they were machines. The banker steps on a banana skin and is made over into a parcel to be deposited by the laws of physics — it doesn't matter whether he was swithering about foreclosure, embezzlement or giving it all up to go paint in the South Seas. So much for free will. Think of determinism as a yellow curve. Mr Calvin the banana man.

In the pub.
"Saatchi? Does that no sound tae you like a Catholic name?"
"Aye. Typical."
Rudi ear-wigging raises his brows.
"Complicated. Take too long to explain."

Outside in a balance of bigots, a drunk one foot in the gutter limping between stanks sings —

Roamin in the gloamin
With a shamrock in my hand,
Roamin in the gloamin
With St Patrick's Fenian Band,
And when the music stops
Fuck King Billy and John Knox,
Oh, it's good to be a Roman Catholic.

"Ah," Rudi says, smiling and nodding to the tune. Pleased with himself. "*Sir* Harry Lauder. Everywhere in this city culture, eh?"

"That's not funny," and folds the sheets once then pinches and squeezes along the fold to put a sharp edge on the rebuke.

"You didn't think the Provost? Not even a wee bit?"

"Kailyard. Misses the target a mile. Like that old 7:84 play that thought a capitalist was a works manager from Cambuslang."

"I don't think it was meant to be anti-capitalist."

"Exactly. Just what I'm saying."

"I think it was just saying it would be nice if the Scots could decide something for themselves for a change."

"I'm not against devolution — at least until we get the Tories out. Been an awful amount of unemployment about these last few years."

"Devolution's like keeping the same old brothel — only you get to pick the colour of the towels. Independence is buying a dog, changing the lock on the front door — and, maybe, if you want what you say you want, telling the moneychangers to get the fuck out of the temple."

"Is that a metaphor?"

"I suppose."

"Like in a poem?"

"If you like."

"So it doesn't have to mean anything."

And walks off.

Ah, well.

"You haven't the least idea who I am," the American said. His
end of the couch sagged under his weight; he was a big man
with something nasal and contemplative in his drawl, a bit like
James Garner. "Not the least damned idea. And I think that's
sad."

"Sorry." I tend to apologise to drunks; if they were dogs, they
would bite me on the ankle. "Were we introduced? Things get
a bit confused."

I stared meaningfully at the perspective of legs and behinds.

"Is that meant to be funny?" His hand jerked so that the
amber liquid swung up under the rim of the glass. "Who killed
John Kennedy?"

"Sorry?"

"I'll bet you know the name of the guy who killed him."

"Lee Harvey Oswald?" Assuming it was the same Kennedy.

"Okay, so that was an easy one. Martin Luther King?"

"Earl Grey?" I wondered. Of course, that was the name of a
tea, but there have been less plausible coincidences.

"You don't want to fool with me," he said. "Ray! James
Earl Ray. He got sentenced to ninety years in a jail in
Mississippi."

"That would be a long time in a jail anywhere," I said. He
stared at me.

"I could tell you all of them. Who killed Robert Kennedy?
Or your own John Lennon? I know them all."

"Who killed Spencer Perceval?" I asked.

"I am not, for Chri'sake, talking yesterday's paper here. I
don't care if some asshole got himself shot in the wrong bed. I
am talking people who mean something in this world."

"Prime Minister. He was Prime Minister. Some time
ago, certainly."

"Of Boogoo-Boogoo Land?" A nasty edge on the voice came
easily to him. "Not in England. Not possible. Doesn't happen
here."

"John Bellingham did it. Shot him in the lobby of the House of Commons. It's not the kind of thing that's likely to happen now," I said wistfully.

"Abraham Lincoln. John Wilkes Booth." He wasn't a man to allow himself to be distracted. "John Garfield — twentieth President. Shot by Charles Guiteau. Did you know any of that?"

"Sirhan Sirhan, the one who shot Bobby Kennedy. It's the repetition, I think, makes the name stick."

"See, you knew. And even if you didn't, you could go and look them up. I mean, they're right there in the books. Go into a library — even in some little pissant country made of sand, I've tried — you'll find them. Isn't anybody can take that away from them."

"Them?"

"The guys who pulled the trigger. What about my name?"

"I'm sorry if I should remember."

"Remember what? Jesus! What I'm saying, my name isn't in any book. But I killed him, and he was as important as John Lennon. Hell of a sight more important than Garfield."

As he gestured, the couch sank under him so that I had to resist rolling down the slope into his arms.

"*Who* was?" I yelped.

"Harry Houdini. You know him."

I agreed.

"Sure you do. Why, fifty years from now I'd bet people will have forgotten Lennon. But not Harry Houdini." His voice was full of inexplicable pride. "He was one hell of a showman. But that isn't why you don't forget him. I don't forget him, not in a hundred years, if anybody's still around. Why? Because he put his life on the line. He said, I can escape from anything you put me into. Bury me, hang me in the air, throw me in the sea, I'll come back. He was saying the grave couldn't hold him. And that's the kind of promise we want to believe."

I wondered if he might be a born-again Christian. It was typical of Peter to arrive when I'd decided not, for the moment, to be rescued.

"Come and talk to me," he said. "You wouldn't believe the perfectly bloody day I've had."

As I went to get up, the American took an unpleasantly firm grip on my elbow. "I killed him and he hasn't come back." I had to give a tug before he released me.

"He said what?" Peter's wife Audrey asked, as I peered back at him through a camouflage of backs and stretching arms.

"He said he killed Houdini."

"He must be drunk," Audrey said, losing interest. "You can't go around boasting about killing people in England — not even foreigners like what's-his-name."

I started to laugh and she looked offended, being less confident than she sounded. "Sorry. It's just that he'd be disappointed to know not everybody remembers Houdini."

"No one killed Houdini," Peter said. All the way back to when we shared the same bench at university, his success had been based less on mother wit than an appetite for facts. "One of his stunts was to have himself tied up and lowered headfirst into a tank of water. He tried it once too often. Instead of getting untied and escaping, he drowned. Your fat man is saying that which is not true."

"He's always doing that," Audrey said bitterly. "I think he makes most of it up."

But Peter contented himself with smiling down at her and changing the subject.

"Rye," I said, "and the weather was glorious. From the tower of the church, there's a fine view of Romney Marshes — smugglers and Dr Syn and all that. And Henry James' house — a bonus to the day. On the way back to the conference, I stopped at an inn just off the road and ate in a timbered room with the odd hen clucking in through the open door. It takes a Scot like me to appreciate the best of England."

"Why ever should that be?" Audrey asked. She wasn't happy.

"Because the best of England is in the past. Unlike us, it's happened to them so recently they don't realise it yet."

"Best?"

". . . The times when you are most yourself. The times when you know you are a member of a community and all its strengths and faults are yours. Some idiosyncratic assertion of its will that marks the character of a nation."

"You're not half so bloody clever as you think you are," Audrey said.

"Sorry?"

"I bloody well hate it when you smile like that."

I realised she was talking to Peter.

She took me by the arm. "Come on. Introduce me to your Houdini man. Upside down in a tank, indeed!"

But the American accepted all of that as true. He wasn't at all ruffled.

"All the same I killed him," he assured us. "A bunch of us had gone backstage. He was tired, but he was always good about seeing College kids. Somebody asked him about this spiritualist medium he'd just shown up as a con artist. It was in all the papers. Harry's mother had died, you see, and he surely wanted to be a believer — but he was just too good a magician not to see through them. He told us, I never stop hoping one of them will be genuine. That made me so mad, I took my best shot and hit him in the belly. I took him by surprise, and I was pretty strong in those days. That's why he couldn't get untied in that tank. I bust something inside him."

"You didn't mean it to happen!" Audrey was startled into good works. The party noise took a quantum jump, and her voice squealed over it. "For you to blame yourself is simply ridiculous."

The fat American gathered us down to him.

"I've seen a soldier cut off a baby's balls, and if he was sitting here with a drink you'd say, nice guy!" He bared his teeth in contempt. "And he was as human as you are. Maybe more — didn't we come out of the swamp and the slime? Maybe you bleeding hearts are some kind of unidentified alien. I wonder if you've dropped here out of some fucking UFO from a star that never had a jungle."

It was Peter who saved the situation.

"Bollocks!" he said. "Houdini died in 1926. That would make the student who punched him eighty something by now. You're having us on."

"1926, is that right?" the fat man asked with a disconcerting smile. "I wasn't even born in 1926." A look of child-like wonder crossed his face as he asked Audrey, "Do you think that's where I went wrong?"

It did seem strange to me that it should be Peter who understood first that it was all an elaborate attempt at being funny. I had never connected him particularly with a sense of humour. I needed another drink.

At some later time, he said to me, "I saw this drunk walking in front of me. In Argyle Street. Yesterday at lunchtime."

"That's one for the diary all right."

"No, listen. He was in an appalling condition, staggering from side to side. So, of course, people were getting out of his way. And these two nuns appeared and as he came towards them they separated and passed on either side of him. And he turned round to me, white as a sheet, and gasped, How did she *do* that?"

"I've heard that before," I said. "As a joke. That's a joke."

"Doesn't mean it couldn't happen," Peter said seriously.

Much later, drifted and cast up in a corner of the room, a handsome woman chose to talk to me. "Not just England, mind you," I said. "It's the same thing with France or Austria or Germany, either Germany." She seemed to be sober, and listened to this with such animation I had to assume it was for the benefit of someone else, perhaps a husband who had found company elsewhere. "In 1914, they'd have laughed if anyone told them the most powerful continent in the world would finish up as a battleground for Russian and American strategists to settle their differences, if it comes to that."

She was smiling, but her eyes had seen something over my shoulder. "I admire what Gorbachev's trying to do, yes." Her face sagged, it was as if a light had been turned off. "Glasnost," she said vaguely.

I glanced at my watch and it was two hours later than I had expected it to be. In a group by the door, a slim girl giggled as she settled back against the man who was helping her on with her coat. With his silver hair and plump jowls he looked like a banker in an old movie.

"I was talking to an American earlier," the handsome woman said miserably. "Such an odd man. He told me he was the pilot of the 'Enola Gay'."

The fat man was still sitting in the same place, holding what might have been the same glass. When he caught my eye, he winked.

"I've met him," I said. "Not a pilot though. I'd put him down as an officer off a nuclear submarine in the Clyde."

"Oh, no," she said. "The 'Enola Gay' dropped the bomb on Hiroshima. He told me about it. I didn't like it, but he wouldn't stop. He said he wasn't a bit sorry."

Looking around, I could see no sign of Peter or Audrey. The party was almost over.

"Don't worry," I told her, "he was joking."

Forgetting to mention Allende

The milk was bubbling over the sides of the saucepan. He rushed to the oven, grabbed the handle and held the pan in the air. The wean was pulling at his trouser-leg, she gripped the material. For christ sake Audrey, he tugged her hand away while returning the saucepan to the oven. The girl went back to sit on the floor, glancing at him as she turned the pages of her colouring book. He smiled: Dont go telling mummy about the milk now eh!

She looked at him.

Aye, he said, that's all I need, you to get into a huff.

Her eyes were watering.

Aw christ.

She looked at him.

You're a big girl now, you cant just . . . he paused. Back at the oven he prepared her drink, lighting a cigarette in the process, which he placed in an ashtray. Along with the drink he gave her two digestive biscuits.

When he sat down on the armchair he stared at the ceiling, half expecting to see it bouncing up and down. For the past couple of hours somebody had been playing records at full blast. It was nearly time for the wean to have her morning kip as well. The same yesterday. He had tried; he had put her down and sat with her, read part of a story: it was hopeless but, the fucking music, blasting out. And at least seven out of the past ten weekdays the same story. He suspected it came from the flat above. Yet it could be coming from through the wall, or the flat below. It was maybe even coming from the other side of the stair — difficult to tell because of the volume, and the way the walls were, like wafer fucking biscuits. Before flitting to the place he had heard it was a good scheme, the houses designed well, good thick walls and that, they could be having a party next door and you wouldnt know unless they came and invited you in. What a load of rubbish. He stared at the ceiling, wondering whether to go and dig out the culprits, tell them the wean was supposed to be having her mid-morning nap. He definitely had the right to complain, but wasnt going to, not yet; it would be daft antagonizing the neighbours at this stage.

Inhaling deeply he got up and wiped the oven clean with a damp cloth. Normally he liked music, any kind. The problem was it was the same songs being played over and over, all the fucking time the same songs — terrible; pointless trying to read or even watch the midday TV programmes. Maybe he was going to have to get used to it: the sounds to become part of the general hum of the place, like the cars screeching in and out of the street, that ice-cream van which came shrieking I LOVE TO GO A WANDERING ten times a night including Sunday.

A digestive biscuit lay crunched on the carpet by her feet.

Thanks, he said, and bent to lift the pieces. The carpet loves broken biscuits. Daddy loves picking them up as well. Come on . . . he smiled as he picked her up. He carried her into the room. She twisted her head from side to side. It was the music.

I know, he said, I know I know I know, you'll just have to forget about it.

I cant.

You can if you try.

She looked at him. He undressed her to her pants and vest and sat her down in the cot, then walked to the window to draw the curtains. The new wallpaper was fine. He came back and sat on the edge of the double bed, resting his hands on the frame of the cot. Just make stories out of the picture, he told her, indicating the wall. Then he got up, leaned in to kiss her forehead. I'll away ben and let you sleep.

She nodded, shifting her gaze to the wall.

You'll have to try Audrey, otherwise you'll be awful tired at that nursery.

Sitting down on the armchair he lifted the cigarette from the ashtray, and frowned at the ceiling. He exhaled smoke while reaching for last night's *Evening Times*. The tin of paint and associated articles were lying at the point where he had left off yesterday. He should have resumed work by now. He opened the newspaper at the sits. vac. col.

The two other children were both boys, in primaries five and six at the local primary school. They stayed in at dinnertime to eat there but normally one would come home after; and if it happened before one o'clock he could send the wee girl back with him to nursery. But neither liked taking her. Neither did daddy for that matter. It meant saying hello to the woman in charge occasionally. And he always came out of the place feeling like an idiot. An old story. It was exactly the same with the headmistress of the primary school, the headmistress of the last primary school, the last nursery — the way they spoke to him even. Fuck it. He got up to make another coffee.

The music had stopped. It was nearly one o'clock. He rushed through to get the wean.

The nursery took up a separate wing within the building of the primary school; only a five-minute walk from where he lived. Weans everywhere but no sign of his pair. He was looking out for them, to see if they were being included in the games yet. He had no worries about the younger one, it was the eldest who presented the problem. Not a problem really, the boy was fine — just inclined to wander about on his tod, not getting involved with the rest, nor making any attempt to. It wasnt really a problem.

The old man with the twins was approaching the gate from the opposite direction; and he paused there, and called: Nice to see a friendly face! Indicating the two weans he continued, The grandkids, what a pair! No twins in the family then all of a sudden bang, two lots of them. My eldest boy gets one pair then the lassie gets another pair. And you know the worrying thing? The old man grinned: Everything comes in threes! Eh?

70

can you imagine it? three lots of twins! That'd put the cat right among the bloody pigeons!

A nursery assistant was standing within the entrance lobby; once she had collected the children the old man said: Murray's the name, John, John Murray.

Tommy McGoldrick.

They shook hands.

I saw you a couple of days ago, the end of last week . . . went on the old man. I was telling my lassie, makes a change to see a friendly face. All these women and that eh! He laughed, and they continued walking towards the gate. You're no long in the scheme then Tommy?

Naw.

Same with myself, a couple of months just, still feeling my way about. I'm staying with the lassie and that, helping her out. Her man's working down in England temporarily. Good job but, big money. Course he's having to put in the hours, but like I was saying to her, you dont mind working so long as the money's there — though between you and me Tommy there's a few staying about here that look as if a hard day's graft would kill them! Know what I mean? naw, I dont know how they do it; on the broo and that and they can still afford to go out and get drunk. Telling you, if you took a walk into that pub down at the shopping centre you'd see half of them were drawing social security. Aye, and you couldnt embarrass them!

They were at the gate. When the old man made as though to continue speaking McGoldrick said, I better be going then.

Right you are Tommy, see you the morrow maybe eh?

Aye, cheerio Mr Murray.

Heh, John, my name's John — I dont believe in the Mr soinso this and the Mr soinso that carry on. What I say is if a man's good enough to talk to then he's good enough to call you by your first name.

He kept a watch for the two boys as he walked back down the road; then detoured to purchase a pie from the local shop, and he put it under the grill to heat up. At 1.20 p.m. he was sitting down with the knife and fork, the bread and butter, the cup of tea, and the letter-box flapped. He had yet to fix up the doorbell.

The eldest was there. Hello da, he said, strolling in.

You no late?

He had walked to the table in the kitchen and sat down there, looking at the pie and stuff. Cold meat and totties we got, he said, the totties were like chewing gum.

What d'you mean chewing gum?

That's what they were like.

Aye well I'd swop you dinners any day of the week . . . He forked a piece of pie into his mouth. What did you get for pudding?

Cake and custard I think.

You think? what d'you mean you think?

The boy yawned and got up from the chair. He walked to the oven and looked at it, then walked to the door: I'm away, he said.

Heh you, you were supposed to be here half an hour ago to take that wean to the nursery.

It wansnt my turn.

Turn? what d'you mean turn? it's no a question of turns.

I took her last.

Aw did you.

Aye.

Well where's your bloody brother then?

I dont know.

Christ . . . He got up and followed him to the door, which could only be locked by turning a handle on the inside, unless a key was used on the outside. As the boy stepped downstairs he called: How you doing up there? that teacher, is she any good?

The boy shrugged.

Ach. He shook his head then shut and locked the door. He poured more tea into the cup. The tin of paint and associated articles. The whole house needed to be done up; wallpaper or paint, his wife didnt care which, just so long as it was new, that it was different from what it had been when they arrived.

He collected the dirty dishes, the breakfast bowls and teaplates from last night's supper. He put the plug in the sink and turned on the hot water tap, shoving his hand under the jet of water to feel the temperature change; it was still a novelty. He swallowed the dregs of the tea, lighted a cigarette, and stacked in the dishes.

A vacuum cleaner started somewhere. Then the music drowned out its noise. He became aware of his feet tapping to the music. Normally he would have liked the songs, dancing music. The wife wouldnt be home till near 6 p.m., tired out; she worked as a cashier in a supermarket, nonstop the whole day. She hardly had the energy for anything. He glanced at the fridge, then checked that he had taken out the meat to defrost. A couple of days ago he had forgotten yet again — egg and chips as usual, the weans delighted of course. The wife just laughed.

He made coffee upon finishing the dishes. But rather than sitting down to drink it he walked to the corner of the room and put the cup down on a dining chair which had old newspaper on its top, to keep it clear of paint splashes. He levered the lid off the tin, stroking the brush across the palm of his hand to check the bristles werent too stiff, then dipped it in and rapidly applied paint to wall. It streaked. He had forgotten to mix the fucking stuff.

Twenty minutes later he was amazed at the area he had covered. That was the thing about painting; you could sit on your arse for most of the day and then scab in for two hours; when the wife came in she'd think you'd been hard at it since breakfast time. He noticed his brushstrokes were shifting periodically to the rhythm of the music. When the letter-box flapped he continued for a moment, then laid the brush carefully on the lid of the tin, on the newspaper covering the chair.

Hi, grinned a well-dressed teenager. Gesturing at his pal he said: We're in your area this morning — this is Ricky, I'm Pete.

Eh, I'm actually doing a bit of painting just now.

We'll only take a moment of your time Mr McGoldrick.

Aye, see I've left the lid off the tin and that.

Yeh, the thing is Mr McGoldrick . . .

His pal was smiling and nodding. They were both holding christian stuff, Mormons probably.

Being honest, said McGoldrick, I dont really . . . I'm an atheist.

O yeh — you mean you dont believe in God?

Naw, no really, I prefer taking a back seat I mean, it's all politics and that, eh, honest, I'll need to get back to the painting.

Yeh, but maybe if you could just spare Ricky and myself one moment of your time Mr McGoldrick, we might have a chat about that. You know it's a big thing to say you dont believe in God I mean how can you know that just to come right out and — hey! it's a big thing — right?

McGoldrick shrugged, he made to close the door.

Yeh, I appreciate you're busy at this time of the day Mr McGoldrick but listen, maybe Ricky and myself can leave some of our literature with you — and you can read through it, go over it I mean, by yourself. We can call back in a day or so, when it's more convenient and we can discuss things with you I mean it seems like a real big thing to me you know the way you can just come right out and say you dont believe in God like that I mean . . . hey! it's a big thing, right?

His pal had sorted out some leaflets and he passed them to McGoldrick.

Thanks, he replied. He shut the door and locked it. He remained there, listening to their footsteps go up the stair. Then he suddenly shook his head. He had forgotten to mention Allende. He always meant to mention Allende to the bastards. Fuck it. He left the leaflets on the small table in the lobby.

The coffee was stone cold as well. He filled the electric kettle. The music blasting; another of these good dancing numbers. Before returning to the paint he lighted a cigarette, stopping off at the bathroom on his way ben.

GEDDES THOMSON

Harry Houdini in Cowcaddens: 1904

The crowd is curiously silent. They fill the street. The constabulary have retired defeated.

It is a male crowd in strangely formal suits and hats. Some of them will be at Buchanan Street Station fourteen years later when the socialist schoolteacher John MacLean arrives from Peterhead prison. They will pull his carriage through the streets of Glasgow. Some of them will be in George Square on Bloody Friday, 1919, when the constabulary attack a workers' demonstration — "to let through a tram" as the *Glasgow Herald* will put it. They have come to catch a glimpse of Houdini, to free themselves perhaps from the chains that bind them to work and wives and children.

Pickpockets are working the crowd. Gently they free wallets and watches from the constrictions of various pockets.

* * * *

At his lodgings in the New City Road Houdini stares out of the window. The old man, who works silently and efficiently at the table behind him, is a Jew, Houdini senses. Houdini is a Jew. The old waiter reminds him of his father.

Houdini swings round and snaps his fingers. When the old man starts to attention with a ghetto gesture, Houdini pulls a piece of cardboard out of the air.

"Could you use a ticket for tonight's show?"

The old man mumbles, "Thank you, Mr Houdini, but I have to work tonight."

Houdini draws back his lips. His broad pale face, his black centre-parted hair, his bright basalt eyes suggest an intelligent

75

panther. "For you, the best seat in the house. I will speak to the manager."

The old man shuffles and studies the pattern of the carpet: "I cannot come. Not tonight."

Houdini gestures, palms upwards. The word "tateh", father, hangs on his tongue. "Why have you never come, in the world, to see me? All things are possible. I have proved it."

The old man looks up. "Will you be able to free Oscar Slater?" he says.

* * * *

Eight carpenters employed by the long-established Glasgow firm of J. and G. Findlay have constructed a box of prime oak. They have challenged Houdini to escape from it. They will nail him into the box and bind it securely with a heavy tarred rope.

* * * *

The crowd stretches from St George's Cross to the Normal School. The trams cannot get through. Inspector James Garvin walks along Great Western Road, wearing his polished badge, to see what the trouble is. A delay in the tramway service is a serious matter. He mentally frames a report to his superiors on this grave incident.

The crowd is densest outside Bostock's Zoo Hippodrome theatre where Houdini will accept the challenge of J. and G. Findlay's eight carpenters. Less than a hundred yards away children with rickets play listlessly in the back-courts of the Maryhill Road tenements.

* * * *

Houdini, in his lodgings, can smell the crowd. He remembers the narrow years of his adolescence on New York's East Side.

A car has arrived to convey him to the theatre, a gleaming maroon Argyle, final flower of Scotland's industrial revolution.

* * * *

"Do you know why they come? They come because you know how to make them think you are going to die."

76

Houdini smiles at his mother across the Atlantic. Tomorrow he will go to Edinburgh and visit the grave of the Great Lafayette. Perhaps he will find something.

In the meantime he will go to the Zoo Hippodrome theatre and lie in the oaken box while J. and G. Findlay's eight carpenters hammer six inch nails above his head. He will escape in fifteen minutes, appear sheened with sweat and minus his shoes in the front of the curtain, and look for the old man in the audience.

* * * *

He will not be there.

ALAN SPENCE

Heart of Glass

Debbie Harry makes me want to cry. Every time I hear her voice it sends shivers down my back. Makes me feel happy and sad at the same time. If you can imagine that. I like everything she sings. Everything. I like 'Dreaming' and 'Atomic' and 'Sunday Girl' and 'Call Me'. Every single and every album track. But best of all I like 'Heart of Glass'. It's absolutely brilliant. Best record ever. *I* think.

> *Once had a love, thought it was a gas*
> *Soon turned out, had a heart of glass.*

Even my dad likes Debbie. At least he always looks up from behind his paper if she's on *Top of the Pops*. And my dad's pretty hard to please when it comes to music.

"There's been nothing since the Beatles," he says. "Absolutely nothing." Then my mum says he's starting to sound middle-aged and that shuts him up. But at least my dad thinks Debbie's all right. Thing is though, he's always calling her Blondie. I keep telling him that's just the name of the group, but he doesn't listen. In one ear and out the other. I suppose Blondie's easier to remember.

The group are good too. Good musicians. But it's Debbie that makes them great.

The lead guitarist's called Chris Stein. He's Debbie's boyfriend. Can you imagine that?

Know who I'd like to be more than anybody else in the world? That's right. I mean, how lucky can you get? Chris Stein. He's the guy with his arm round her on the cover of 'Eat to the

Beat'. He's not even all that good-looking, is he?

Not that I can talk. About being good-looking I mean! I haven't got a girlfriend at all. I know I'm only fourteen. But . . . it's just not that easy.

There's this girl in my class at school. Her name's Moira. She's got blonde hair too. Really nice looking. She's not like Debbie, but she couldn't be, could she? I once got up the courage to ask Moira to dance, at the school disco. They were playing 'Heart of Glass'. It was like being in Heaven. The song and the lights and Moira's soft scent and everything.

Thing is, when the record was finished that was it. I couldn't think of anything brilliant to say. In fact I couldn't think of anything to say at all. I just felt really awkward and stupid.

Moira went back to her seat and the next thing she was up dancing with this big guy from fifth year. He ended up seeing her home.

That's the thing. I mean what chance have you got being fourteen when all the girls your own age are going out with guys of sixteen or seventeen! What are you supposed to do? Go out with a ten-year-old? Get had up for baby-snatching. Fourteen!

I read in this magazine that Debbie is thirty-four. It seems ridiculous. I mean, my *mother* is thirty-four. And I suppose my mother's not bad looking really. For a mother. If you know what I mean. It's just hard to believe she's the same age as Debbie. Thirty-four.

And I'm fourteen, and I wish I wasn't.

Being fourteen is rubbish. Nobody knows what it's like. Nobody remembers. They treat you like a kid and expect you to behave like a grown-up. RUBBISH.

> *In between*
> *What I find is pleasing and I'm feeling fine*
> *Love is so confusing there's no peace of mind.*

You know, my pal Eddie doesn't think Debbie's all that great. But then he hasn't got much taste. He likes Olivia Newton-John for Godsake. He's got a big poster of her up on his wall. From

Grease. She's all in black leather, trying to look sexy.

I guess I remember her from TV shows when I was a kid. Dancing like a stookie. Singing sweetie-pie duets with Cliff Richard. Pretty disgusting really. So *English*.

Debbie's just in a different class. She's got this *hard* look. Sort of glassy-eyed. Looks like she's in her own world. Doesn't care about *anything*. And yet sometimes you look at her face and she could be sixteen. She's young and old at the same time. I've got a great poster of her. Just a big close-up of her face. Beautiful.

This guy was selling them outside the Apollo the night of the concert at Hogmanay. I couldn't believe it when I heard Blondie were coming. Queued up all night to get a ticket.

I had to go on my own too. Tried to talk Eddie into coming, but he couldn't be bothered. Said it was too expensive and he wasn't all that keen on Blondie anyway. I told you. No taste at all.

The night of the concert I went into town early and spent ages hanging around. New Year coming and everybody getting tanked up already. Big queues outside the licensed grocers. You know that *empty* feeling that sort of hangs about the place. New Year. But all I could think about was that Blondie were in town. Debbie was in Glasgow! I suppose I was hoping I might somehow bump into her. Stupid really. I mean, how could it happen? And if it did, what would I say to her?

"Hello there. How ye doin'? Ah think yer great and ah love all yer records. Especially 'Heart of Glass'."

> *Lost inside adorable illusion*
> *And I cannot hide*

It felt strange, going to the concert on my own. I once went to the pictures on my own. Took an afternoon off school. There were me and three other people in the whole place. Felt really creepy. If you laughed you could hear your own voice ringing out in the dark. Then there was the weird feeling of coming out and finding it was still daylight. The Blondie concert wasn't like that of course. The place was packed. But even though there were hundreds of people, I still felt funny.

I still felt *alone*. Waiting for it to start was worse than waiting for Scotland to run on to the park at Hampden.

The atmosphere built up and up. Then the curtain opened and there she was. Debbie, for real, up there in a striped dress and yellow tights, bouncing around in the bright, bright light, singing 'Hanging on the Telephone'.

I had a great seat, four rows from the front. Everybody was really excited. Before I knew what I was doing, I rolled up my Rangers scarf and threw it on to the stage.

And later on the most incredible thing happened. While she was singing 'Pretty Baby', Debbie picked up the scarf. *My* scarf! She wrapped it round herself then threw it into the audience. There was a scramble down at the front and the scarf disappeared. I couldn't get near it. The bouncers would have had me out on my ear if I'd even tried.

Towards the end of the concert the stage lights went down. There was just a kind of strobe-light flashing. The keyboards and percussion went into a slow build-up, the introduction I knew so well. I felt tingly all over. Electric. Then the spotlight was on Debbie, dancing to the front of the stage, belting out 'Heart of Glass'. I was nearly in tears.

On the way out of the hall afterwards, I saw Moira. She was with the big guy from fifth year she'd got off with at the disco. They didn't see me, and I think I was glad. He looks a bit like Chris Stein.

The town centre was even more depressing now. The closer it got to New Year, the more folk were roaming about, loud and drunk.

Back home, my dad said he'd seen some of the concert on TV. He said I should have stayed in and watched it; saved my money. But it's not the same. No atmosphere. Same with football.

"Did ye see her with a Rangers scarf?" I asked.

"Must have missed that bit," he said.

"Well anyway," I said. "It was mine. Ah threw it on the stage."

"Hope ye don't expect me to buy ye a new one," said my mother.

By the time the bells were going, the house was full of uncles and aunties and cousins, the people next door, the old wifie downstairs. Happy New Year!

I hate New Year at the best of times, but tonight for some reason it was worse than ever. Before I knew where I was I was crying. My mother saw me before I could get out of the room.

"What's the matter son?" she said.

"Nothing," I said. "Nothing."

How could I tell her it was Debbie, and Moira, and 'Heart of Glass', and my scarf, and not being Chris Stein, and not being grown-up, and not being a kid, and being fourteen, and the stupid New Year, and *everything*.

DAVID NEILSON

In the Desert

"Thae blisters is actually away," said McLeish, grasping his left foot in his hand and bending it round. His feet were sculptures, all interesting planes and angles. He gazed down at them as he set them carefully, like things brand new, on the groundsheet.

"They'll start again when we move," said Farquharson. "Ye canny help getting blisters walkin through this."

"It's amazin how yir feet get manky, intit?" McLeish's voice echoed under the campbed as he twisted his head down to look for his sash. He came up again and examined his toes. "Ah dono wherr ma toenails start any merr."

Farquharson brushed aside the flap and looked out. Over the dormitory tents the sun burned white, so fierce, so incandescent that the very points of weapons gleamed no brighter than the sky behind. Camels in the open, a few standing as easily as the others knelt, shimmered at the edges against the haze.

"Are we gaun roon tae see wee Calum?" he said. "He'll be gaun aff his nut."

"Dono," said McLeish. "Whiddye think?"

"It's no particularly chancy."

Farquharson started suddenly.

"Lissn," he said. "It's the wee man. He's gaun roon aw the tents."

He jumped again. The subaltern's head, tilted alarmingly and leaning in from the side, had appeared beside him.

"If yiz kin make it, boays," he said, forcing Farquharson back inside the tent, "wiv arranged a wee meetin. Seems to be a problem. This patter that the grub's rotten ur somethin. Gie it five minutes."

The head vanished.

"Ahv never seen his hale boady," said Farquharson.

"This whit aw this is aboot? Wee Calum gettin the jail an that?"

"Ten tae wan he wis up complainin. He's awright tae dinner time and aw he does then is moan." Farquharson stuck his head out again. "They're no exactly rushin oot fur this, by the way."

"He's goat nae conversation," said McLeish, lacing up his sandal. "Aw he kin talk aboot is God."

Number One stood on a hillock, trampling the last grass of the wadi. From time to time he would take scraps of parchment from his plaid, ruffle through them, and crush them away again.

He was a square-headed little man, the angularity of his skull accentuated by a haircut that passed for austere even by the standard of the corps. His voice, no less than his body, was unusual, since he used strange vowels that suggested a place of birth, or manufacture, somewhere at the other end of the earth from that of most of the army; but his stance was even odder, for when he spoke his frame exercised a wild dynamic, so that at one moment his head dipped below the slanting line of his shoulders, while at another, his neck extending and the metallic resonance of his tones growing more brazen, his arms would swing out and his knees lock straight and rigid. Then he would twist through an unforeseeable angle, and, close to the point of emphasis in the sentence, his voice would swell in a crescendo.

The cook, standing at a little distance, though well within earshot, glowered forbiddingly, and his apprentice, who shouldered the handle of a heavy pot, looked vacantly around the slowly gathering crowd. Beside him was a smaller boy, with hair cut oddly on one side, holding a scrap of paper; there was a camel trainer in a long white gown, and two orderlies carrying sacks of rubbish which they deposited in front of them before straightening up and folding their arms in order to listen to Number One. McLeish was almost swaggering as they joined the circle, since he could now walk without limping, but his step became cautious as he grasped Farquharson's arm, pulling him behind people who were bigger than they were so that they could laugh.

"Is that gauney be a cardinal?"

"Looks like it," said Farquharson. "The boss gave him a special form."

Number One's prospects were considerable. The Bishop of Strathclyde, in his palace beside the cathedral church of St Senga, was known to be failing. Old enough to have seen the advent of the imperial line (though wise enough not to have been openly of Sammy the Glaikit's party at the cataclysm known as the battle of Anniesland), the Bishop was now of old-fashioned sentiment; and, in age, he had been heard to mutter in terms of grudging respect for the Bad Samaritan.

Among his greatest irritations was Number One's subtle placing of agents in the Chapter House of St Senga's, from whose vestries emanated numberless paeans, and even more numerous formal motions, in praise of the dread figure who dominated the west of Scotland, and was the terror of Europe. It was insupportable that this work should take precedence over tasks of real importance, such as restoring the shrine of St Senga to the magnificence it had enjoyed in the time of the kings. For in these same precincts, sullied now by presumptuous statuary, St Senga had collated leaves of the Glorious Gleanings calendar in her great calling of redemption for the Bulgars; and there the fatal cupboard, stacked imprudently on the upper shelves, pending the resolution of a carriage dispute, had toppled on her. Her extenuated form had, ever since, been preserved in the manner of a scroll, and was alternately venerated and catalogued; now, as Patron Saint of Diarists, and with the diocesan *nihil obstat,* she was exhibited in leap years. From time to time working parties turned over the possibility of maintaining the relic in the style of a codex, but the technical problems had remained insuperable.

"Mr McLeish!" It was a boy's voice; an excited voice.

"Hullo," said McLeish, looking round. The boy with the paper was holding it up and waving it. "OK, let's have it."

By now a few cowled figures, thrusting out poles with collecting boxes for the St Vincent de Paul Society, had placed themselves at the edges of the gathering. The Junior Marauders, McLeish recalled, were on a cross-country run, but a few of the militia were standing around leaning on spears. Number One himself was looking, by turns, in a variety of directions.

McLeish held his hand out for the note, took it, and unfolded it, looking at the brown-haired boy who all the while was scrutinising Farquharson and his ancient, cracked, grey leather breastplate. Farquharson bent over him and adopted an air of the utmost sternness.

"Allegations have been made," he said, in a deep, wild voice, jabbing his forefinger in the air, "and woe betide the alligators!"

The boy looked at McLeish.

"Dear R. McLeish," McLeish read, "please check this boay's ears. L. Cameron Duguid, Principal Medical Officer."

"Right," said McLeish. He held out his right foot and said, "In precisely fifteen seconds ma big toe is gauney faw aff." The boy stared. McLeish grasped his head firmly and peered.

"Just about time to start," said Number One, craning his neck to see over the edge of the crowd. "Well, looking round, I must say that this appears to be one in the eye for those Jeremiahs who've been telling us that we don't have a free flow of information in the corps."

As McLeish looked up, squinting into the light, he noticed the subaltern standing some distance away, behind a low tent, his arms folded.

"OK," he said. "Don't poke anythin in them."

The boy sat down on the sand, and, in a moment, stretched himself out. McLeish was vaguely conscious of Number One's voice, and he prodded the boy.

"Ye canny sleep the noo," he said.

"It's all right," said the voice, finally breaking through. "I don't mind if he dozes."

McLeish looked up.

"It isny that," he said. "He wullny sleep the night."

Number One looked round again.

"The first matter to which I must address myself," he said, "is the apparent dissent of which such great play has been made this afternoon.

"Or not dissent." He had hunched himself up and was coiled to launch himself at the audience. The top half of his body sprang, though his feet remained planted. His plaid flew. "For what we are dealing with here is what few would hesitate to call — and notice that I do not, at this stage, commit myself — the most desperate treason."

The revelation was accompanied by the shooting of his left hand into the air, with the thrusting of a finger.

"He is an absolute madman," muttered McLeish from the side of his mouth.

"A madman," said Farquharson quietly, looking round in case anyone had noticed.

"What, indeed, can we call it, when the most reckless and abandoned elements put it about that some members of the team are failing to pull their weight?"

Number One pointed at a slingshot carrier in the front row.

"What would you call it?"

The man remained still.

"Yes," said Number One, "a criminal insinuendo."

"He's away wi it," said McLeish, straining not to move his lips. "Giein wee Calum the jail."

Number One was pointing backwards, over his head, at the horizon.

"It is our very comrades-in-arms that are being maligned," he said. "It's all very well, all very reasonable, to nit-pick about shortcomings, the inevitable gremlins in the management decision process. But I can issue this challenge, with unbridled confidence, to the nit-pickers. Where would we be, I put it to you, without these decisions?"

"Sunny Govan," Farquharson whispered, lowering his brows and looking attentive.

"Came up through supplies," said McLeish. "Look at him."

Farquharson noticed that a few Junior Marauders who must have been excused the cross-country run were scaling a ballista in the mobile pound a few tents away. The guards had probably been called over to form part of the audience.

"Whit aboot the tripe soup?"

The meeting was suddenly alive. The camel trainer, instead of struggling with his camel, thwacked it behind the ear, and it was still.

Farquharson nudged McLeish.

"I'm going to answer that," said Number One, "but first I'd like to say a word or two about supplies. Because one of the most distinguishing characteristics of this campaign has been the regularity, indeed the unfailing consistency, of the services section and its capacity to deliver. In the particular case I'm coming to here — because I'm coming to it — no deficiency has ever been found in the quantity of nourishing broth available to the ranks.

"Just pause for a moment to consider the logistics of this operation. It's no mean feat, let me tell you, to co-ordinate the resources of a dozen centres, and manhandle them over the inhospitable wastes, harried by lawless brigands, and prey to heat and thirst. And if you ask an old hand they'll tell you that after a week or two straining at the hawsers, muscles cracking, joints aflame, that no concoction on earth is more revivifying than the wholesome potage that dietetic science has deemed miracle soup.

"So, whatever flies remain to be ironed out of the ointment, it will be necessary to take a dim view of any catering criticisms within the present timescale. In fact, there will be little for it but to threaten dissidents with confinement. And if this appears harsh to anyone, let them recall that at this very instant our secret operative, moving indistinguishably among the desert tribes, accepted as one of their own, is risking life and limb for the success of this campaign. I don't suppose wee Davey McBride — which is, of course, a codename — is worried about what he's having for his dinner. Do you see him concerned about whether he'll be getting stuffed partridge and canapés? He'd just be glad to give thanks to his Maker sitting down to a steaming bowl of tripe soup."

Farquharson prodded McLeish again, and caught Number One's eye at the same time. Gesturing in such a way as to indicate that he was just going over to see why people were climbing on a ballista, he grabbed McLeish by the nape of the neck and fell out of the gathering.

"He's really gung ho on the tripe soup," said McLeish.

Farquharson looked at the sand as they walked, smiled a little, and shook his head.

"Jist jump," McLeish shouted. "Dive. Heid furst intae the wadi."

He turned to Farquharson. "Is that other bampot awright?"

Craig was lying under the ballista making sounds like ahyah, ahyah.

"We kin get ye a bucket a icewatter," McLeish shouted up to Mark, who was gripping an upright, "or send tae Alexandria fur a ladder. Whiddye fancy, the bucket?"

"Naw, naw," said Mark.

"It's cool," said Farquharson. "Ye kin hardly smell the tripe." He bent over Craig. "This is superb practice. Therr a hunner an fifty fitter up the road."

"Ahyah," said Craig.

McLeish was looking, as he was always forced to, at the rough stencilling on the base of the ballista, staining the pine like faded blood.

THIS BALLISTA IS THE PROPERTY OF STRATHCLYDE LIBRARIES DEPARTMENT.
If it is wilfully or carelessly damaged or lost,
it must be replaced by the borrower.

"Stencilled signatures look funny, don't they?" said McLeish. "Forbes Colquhoun, Director of Libraries."

"Ah didny know that wis a library function," said Farquharson. "Dye need a special ticket or anythin? Gauney haud still a minute till ah see if this spleen is ruptured?"

"Naw," said McLeish, "this is an Aitcheson B. Only model they made durin the projectile overspend. Could ye keep hangin on in there? Wiv sent fur Shields the Grampian alpinist.

He's gauney hack a path doon wi his icepick."

Farquharson looked up, shaking his head.

"He's fae Tarbert," he said.

"It's cool," said McLeish. "He still gets the *Mornin Star*."

"Funny thing tae caw them, that, intit?" said McLeish. They were sitting on packs outside the tent, watching the blue fade at the distant peaks, the mountains wash into thin, jagged bands of peach and plum.

Farquharson looked at the greasy rim of his bowl.

"Whit?" he said.

"Junior Marauders," said McLeish.

"Ah dono, how?"

"Well, thirz nae senior wans, is therr?"

Farquharson looked at him.

"Comin roon?" he said.

They scuffed their way through the dust. Half hidden behind a trolley, the subaltern was inspecting ladlefuls of tripe soup.

"Tellin ye," said Farquharson.

The Junior Marauders were scattered along the path. Brown, thin, they lay motionless as Farquharson and McLeish passed.

"Jist as well," said Farquharson. "If they hid any Senior Marauders we'd hiv tae organise trainin courses fur them as well."

"Wherr we headed?"

"Review area," said Farquharson. "Jist look fur a tent wi bars oan the windaes."

"Thirz a special form fur complaints," said the adjutant, unfolding a camp chair for McLeish. Farquharson squatted on a low stool, his knees jutting almost to his breastbone. "Ah mean, ahv never actually seen wan but ah know they hiv them. Here, is it cauld in here ur am ah jist imaginin it?"

"It's OK," said McLeish, settling. "Fine. Is therr any special forms fur bail, ur appeals, ur anythin?"

"No actually as such. It's certainly an idea. Ah seem tae mind that somebody wis gauney suggest it in the newsletter."

"Influential, that," said Farquharson.

"It is cauld in here," said the adjutant. "Thir aye leavin thae flaps open. No in the actual detention areas, right enough. Naw, it's in the hand a the gods. If the guy that does Birds a the Desert still has his septic finger, yir laughin. Lissn, did ye get yir leaflet a visitin times?"

"The winter solstice, basically?" said Farquharson.

The adjutant was looking in a small chest.

"Sorry," he said, surfacing. "There is a thermometer here. A vial a St Senga's blood. If the workin environment isny sixteen point five inside an oor it liquifies."

"Is it really aw that serious a charge?"

"Well, it's goat serious sides. The actual charge is that yir man, wee Calum, did shout cahoochieburgers outside the mess tent, putting the lieges into a state of fear an alarm."

"It wis the burgers that pit them intae a state of fear an alarm," said McLeish.

"Naw," said Farquharson, laying a hand on McLeish's arm, "whit evidence is there that any contretemps actually ensued?"

"It's jist it coulda," said the adjutant. "The guys are jumpy." His grey eyebrows rose and looked from side to side without really taking his eyes off them. "Ah shouldnae be tellin ye this, but ye probbli know. We're jist waitin fur word fae wee Davey McBride. He speaks the native dialects as if born to them and moves imperceptibly among the Bedouin. It's as close as that."

"But there wis nae damage," said Farquharson. "Naebdi actually refused cabbage or anythin."

"It's a sensitive political situation," said the adjutant. He moved his head closer to theirs and half-whispered, nodding as he spoke. "Ye know they didny get tae the cash an carry in Alexandria."

"Ye'll need tae let him oot," said McLeish. "We canny dae withoot wee Calum. They caw us the Three Musketeers."

"Are ye inseparable?" said the adjutant.

"Naw," said McLeish, "we run aboot stabbin people."

"Could we no even see him?" Farquharson broke in. "Take him his tea or whit?"

"Ahv a big bowl a tripe soup right here," said McLeish.

"Ye better forget it," said the adjutant. "There's some offences that happen tae be numero uno, an this is the main wan."

"It's that political?" said Farquharson.

"Aye. Therr some people ye canny cross."

"Whit'll happen tae him?"

"If he's lucky he'll get drivin a siege engine fur the Junior Marauders."

"Wherr is he the noo?"

"Under automatic guard."

"Aw naw." Farquharson put his hands over his eyes and scowled. McLeish shook his head and looked away. "No wan a thae things?"

The adjutant nodded.

"Ah thought the normal arrangement," said McLeish, "wis that the monkeys were in the cages an the humans looked at thaim."

"It's slashed the wages bill," said the adjutant.

"It's probbli slashed wee Calum," said McLeish. "Thae things are psychotic."

"Don't say too much aboot them either," said the adjutant. "They're politically sexy at the moment."

McLeish lifted a hand. Farquharson, as he got ready to grab him, noticed the adjutant shift.

Then the screech hit them, the shearing overtone on a rasping growl, like a length of iron ripped through by a metal saw.

The adjutant jerked.

"It is cauld in here," he said. "Ahl jist shut this flap."

Farquharson moved first, grunting as he heaved himself from the stool. As he tripped over a sack, he dived at the opening and felt something cold and sharp whip past his face. He fell in a dusty odour of canvas, and panicked, tugging at his caught ankle.

McLeish was above him, shouting incoherently, thrashing against the tent pole at the side of the flap.

Farquharson doubled quickly and thrust back his leg, knocking over something that was yelling, "Ye'll break it! Ye'll break it!"

McLeish was wrapped in a black fury which gripped him about the waist and was throttling him at the same time. Working on to his knees, Farquharson clasped his hands and battered the monkey below the skull.

It screeched again, a neuralgic screech, and released an upturning left paw, going for pole-mounted offensive weapons, as was Farquharson.

McLeish wrenched his head aside and grasped the monkey's right with both hands.

Farquharson tore the grid from the tent pole, scattering the short swords. As he grabbed the nearest, tightening his grip, he was struck, blindingly, and tumbled, the left side of his face on fire.

He shook himself, and saw McLeish collapsing, headed by a black blur. The monkey swung round the pole, catching a sword in the lower paw it had used on Farquharson, and let go.

It flipped over. The sword was raised in its upper right, and it screeched again, higher and more piercing, the scream of gear on gear.

There was, Farquharson became aware, a dagger sticking from its lower left paw. It crouched still and threatening, whirring down to a creak. It grimaced haltingly, uttered a croaking "Eep", and stopped.

McLeish was out, bleeding at the nose, but breathing. Farquharson very slowly brought his swordpoint around.

"It's OK. Scratch wan clockwork monkey."

The voice came from the floor. Farquharson turned his head. The subaltern, half in the door flap, was lifting himself on to his elbow.

"Jist as well ah showed ma face," he said.

Farquharson nodded.

"Well flung, sir," he breathed. "Thae things are mental."

"Ah know," said the subaltern. "Mind the left index toe, but don't let oan."

He scrambled to his knees.

"Were ye jist poppin yir heid roon the door?" said Farquharson.

"Naw," said the subaltern. "There's an immediate amnesty fur embdi in fabrication. Wee Davey McBride's sent in a signal fae Cairo. They've clocked Robert the Vole."

"Is that right?"

The subaltern nodded.

"Recognition classes to be set up first thing," he said.

"An wee Calum can go?"

"Aye. Therr a consignment of Anniesland Crosses needed as soon as possible. He's gauney be busy." He turned and stuck his head through the flap. "Lissn, hiv you goat a clockwork monkey incident form?"

RONALD FRAME

Incident in Le Lavandou

The view was not as Miss Simm remembered it. The plane trees must have been the same ones — their tops were just visible — but white buildings pressed in on the old streets from all sides and she could see no plan to the town. There must be one — she might find it down at street level — but the longer she looked the more confused she felt she was becoming.

She finished dressing in front of the wardrobe mirror, with the open balcony-doors and the blue Riviera sky behind her. She thought, perhaps if I'd lived here I should scarcely have been conscious of all the changes in half a century?

She stood straightening her skirt, pulling at the cuffs of her blouse, telling herself how different it was from Largs. *I'm here, I managed the journey after all, there's life in the old girl yet.*

But when the wardrobe door and the mirror swung back on creaking hinges the view and the confidence disappeared, and she felt elderly and rather foolish and terribly Scottish in her tweeds as she looked about her to find the canvas shoes she'd brought with her as a concession to the town's hot streets.

* * * *

Madame Lépront stood drinking her coffee at the little filigreed balcony, watching the patterns of life on the streets far beneath her. It had been her idea that the junk-filled attic of the villa could be turned into a commodious, sunny apartment, and the result justified all the hard graft of long ago: a quiet, forgotten spot high above people's heads, easily kept in order, cool in summer when the shutters were closed and, with its low ceilings and because the rooms underneath were always occupied by tenants, not too expensive to heat in winter. Bright and airy, it suited widowhood. Few people suspected that anyone lived up here among the rafters, which even the pigeons had abandoned by the time they got down to the conversion work.

She took mouthfuls of the hot milky coffee. She swallowed it noisily, in gulps, and heard herself. Her manners had suffered a bit since Guy's death. When she'd married she'd had to get used to the French way of attacking food with such relish, and now nearly fifty years later she couldn't undo herself of the habit. She might have passed for "Made in France".

Madame Lépront always enjoyed the early heat of the day and she liked to feel it warming the stone of the balcony under her bare feet and the roof tiles she leaned her back against. Later on in the day she wasn't so comfortable with it. She stayed indoors, or she would make her forays in the car; if it happened she was meeting someone and she had no choice about being out, she kept as much as possible to the shade. About six o'clock the sun lost its spite and she reappeared on the balcony to have a drink, whatever there was on the sideboard. A couple of hours later the sun turned to the colour of a blood-orange as it sank slowly behind Africa. The sky would have a mysterious greenish tinge some nights; on others it would suddenly catch fire from the sun, flaming to crimson, and she would watch as other colours composed themselves around the red-hot core, vermilion, couleur de rose, then lighter fleshier pinks, cooling to topaz and Indian yellow and lemon on the extremities.

* * * *

The heat, thought Miss Simm, the heat: that would have been the worst of it, I should never have adjusted.

But the skies, *they* would have been something to see, evening after evening. Maybe I would have taken up sketching, water-colours, pastels, gouache: maybe even proved myself quite adept.

Maybe.

* * * *

Indoors again — the coffee doing its work and pepping her up after her night's deep sleep — Madame Lépront dressed.

Summerwear was straightforward: a pale cotton shift and espadrilles, it couldn't have been easier.

She combed her hair back over her ears, and applied a very little, very discreet liner to her eyes.

She looked hard at herself. Her face had become thinner with the years, and longer if that was possible: or perhaps it was because she only saw French faces that she viewed her own differently now. Decades of sun had bleached her hair, so that she was scarcely able to recognise the dark-fringed woman in photographs, posed with her mother and father and her sister and two brothers. The sun had also toughened her skin and lined it, and sometimes she smiled rather sadly when she told people about her foreign youth and her "peaches-and-cream" complexion, as the term used to be.

This morning, though — thinking positively — she felt that her appearance had an *authenticity* about it which it never used to have. She was wholly herself, she didn't need to satisfy other people's expectations of how she should look. The longer she lived, the simpler the presentation and final version of herself became. For that she thanked her years in France, now — unbelievably — two-thirds of her life.

* * * *

"Une tasse de thé, s'il vous plait. Comment? Un thé? Très bien. Pour moi seule. Thé de chine. Merci."

Miss Simm had never felt comfortable with such an extrovert language. Passing the simplest remark involved contorting your face to pronounce some absurd, indecently sensuous-sounding hotch-potch of syllables.

At least the waiter nodded his head: but curtly, Miss Simm thought. Frumpy British types obviously weren't worth humouring. No tip for *you*, she decided, and the little revenge in prospect reassured her.

Miss Simm placed her day-old *Telegraph* on top of the table, and she laid her room key on top of it.

What would her friends be doing at home, she wondered?

Probably wondering what *she* was doing with herself and why on earth should she want to hive herself off to the South of France at *her* age. They'd be puzzling about that, and about the other matters that preoccupied them, which filled their days and hers because there was no getting away from them: annuities, the sloth and miserliness of the faceless dispensers of company pensions, the tardiness of lawyers dealing with a cousin's will, a shares statement, the red print demand on an electricity bill which had already been paid, the new rates estimate, an accountant's fee for offices rendered, the state of the roses in the landscaped gardens of the block where they lived.

How odd that she was suddenly feeling so disengaged about it. But, she thought, maybe in another couple of days' time I shall have reverted again?

Normally she didn't go on holiday alone, she went with one of her neighbours, or with someone she'd worked with in the manufacturers' agent's business her brother had built up and which he had "invited" her to lend her services to — and the conversation wherever their travels took them would inevitably return to home, and to the past. This time the past that concerned her was known only to herself and to her twin cousins in Strathpeffer, the three of them being the sole survivors of that family group who'd come south in 1936. And perhaps — just perhaps — it was still known to *him*: the Frenchman she'd never been able to forget even though she couldn't have described his face to save her life and whose own life had been more or less a mystery to her, then and ever since.

* * * *

Madame Lépront enjoyed her privacy and independence. No one here saw her comings and goings, even though the rest of the building was occupied. The villa was hers now — it had come to Guy through the will of an aunt — and perhaps she was allowed her privacy out of respect, she couldn't be sure. "La Châtelaine" and all that.

She drew an income from the tenants, here and in several other properties which Guy — with his professional land-agent's eye and sixth sense — had had the good sense to buy.

Nowadays she was a bona fide businesswoman: at this comparatively late juncture in her life she had the self-assurance and the financial say-so — and, still, the mental and physical stamina — to be able to badger lawyers and accountants, and she made it a point of honour not to be brow-beaten or fobbed off by any of them. She could be quite charming when she chose to be, but that never obscured the fact that her husband's death had turned her into a very determined and very knowing woman where the practicalities of commerce were concerned. People could tell by the authority of her body walking into a room, the set of her face, the shine in her eyes. She'd had to work at it, but now she wouldn't have wanted to be any other way than she was.

She closed her front door behind her, heard the lock turn, then she hurried down the three flights of stairs with a swiftness of foot that she knew belied her years.

* * * *

Well, at seventy-two one presumes there just isn't the energy — the vim — left, thought Miss Simm. Not for gallivanting off to foreign parts. Even if this isn't exactly gallivanting, not quite. And of course these aren't just *any* run-of-the-mill foreign parts . . .

She crumpled the paper napkin and, after hesitating, let it drop on to her plate of croissant crumbs.

She couldn't have taken to French breakfasts, she was quite positive about that. Too much fuss for nothing. And why did croissants always *have* to have that greasy feel to them?

Better off with her Bran Buds, and one slice of wholemeal toast, and the Frank Cooper's, and Algie's no-nonsense Ceylon tea.

"Better off as I am." The words were on the tip of her tongue to say, but she realised there was no one to hear if she were to open her mouth and say them, and she also wondered if she was really the person best qualified to judge.

The words lacked, somehow, *conviction*.

* * * *

No one in Le Lavandou was certain how old Madame Lépront was, but it was general knowledge that she'd first come to the town in the 1930s, when she was someone else, the younger daughter of a foreigner and his wife on holiday here — a businessman, a "tea merchant" hadn't she said, *un marchand de thé*: when she had been a pale and fragile young woman, shy beneath her fringe of dark hair.

The most precise of her neighbours guessed that now she must be seventy or thereabouts: "guessed", Madame Lépront was perfectly aware. (In warmer climes, she knew, it's often easier to make a riddle of numerals — sixty-five, seventy, seventy-five — among faces prematurely wrinkled and veined and stoically smiling under their uniform tans. In sunshine you can dress to virtually any age you choose: other people are more charitable about any sartorial miscalculations and errors of taste, it's merely amusing — for a brief time — then assimilated into the everyday way of things. Madame Lépront realised that public opinion was decided that on the whole she dressed with sense but also with some "chic", in styles that would have looked just as well worn by a woman half her age. It was a verdict that gave her much secret satisfaction.)

Guy Lépront's widow stood in the downstairs hallway opening her morning's mail. Sunlight flooded through the open double-doors and washed over the checker-board of black and white tiles. Vaguely, as she read, she was conscious of the heady brew of the garden's perfumes: pine, floribunda roses, rosemary, orange blossom, the inevitable lavender that the town was named after. The fragrance and the heat lapping round her always made her feel well-disposed even when her correspondence was about financial business and she was required to make some brisk mental calculations there and then. The men she dealt with in the business line were there for a purpose, they had specific duties which she was paying them to perform and she refused to be intimidated or confused by their manner: when they wrote to her they were required to express themselves, please, with particular clarity. *"Elucidez, s'il vous plaît. Avec concision."*

Madame Lépront bundled the assortment of letters and

postcards into her bag, shut the clasp, and dropped the bag into her basket. Walking down the front steps and across the gravel, out of the villa's shadow, she felt buoyant and prepared for whatever the day might be bringing her.

* * * *

Back upstairs in her bedroom, Miss Simm debated whether or not she should take her plastic mackintosh and rain-mate with her. Yes, she decided, yes, I *shall* take them.

It always paid to be on the safe side. Better safe than sorry. And who knew more about the safe and sensible and least hazardous way of living this life than herself?

* * * *

On cloudless mornings when she felt like walking on the balls of her feet, Madame Lépront could believe she'd taken full and proper advantage of all the opportunities that had come her way in this life. She'd allowed life to take her, not always where she'd been expecting to go, but where it seemed to have determined that she should be taken. Life's plans for her hadn't been the same as her family's, and she'd had to persist in the face of their opposition. She could have heeded the puritan designs of her father and mother and the clamouring maiden aunts and made of herself whatever they would have decided according to the models of their class and country: a stainless wife-to-be for a redoubtable fiancé, or a meek and modest stay-at-home daughter, or — had they been willing to allow her a little more independence, plus an allowance — she might have become an untested, prim-mouthed young woman settling prematurely into spinsterhood in a decent community of like souls.

Instead she lived on the Côte d'Azur and in sunshine: and if there must be shadows, they were no threat to her, not now after fifty years. When her children and grandchildren quizzed her gently about her past, she let them see that it was neither here nor there to her — concealing nothing that they wanted to know — but that really she preferred to think of the life she had shared with *them* as her true history. She had given much thought to the past, however, in a more abstract sense. She'd often wondered if people's lives don't all contain some emotional apogee, some heightened and climactic omega of experience, its highwater mark, which might occur at any point — early or late — and turns into an epiphany, a moment of revelation. One of two consequences ensues from the event: either everything else that follows proves a falling-off and tailing-away and nothing is ever felt so intensely again — or the opposite happens, the incident becomes a pointer to possibilities that previously hadn't occurred to you and you turn towards them, freshly confident and cast in a new frame of mind.

Confident, but with the uncomfortable consciousness of betrayal. For hadn't she committed the one heinous and finally unpardonable crime: she'd left the country where she'd grown up and its northern climes, she'd abandoned its morality and the bracing winds and grey days of soft Atlantic drizzle for marriage and the white Mediterranean light and empty Latin noons and green African twilights of this lavender town, Le Lavandou?

* * * *

After breakfast Miss Simm stood in the hallway of the hotel consulting a map on the wall. Unconcerned voices passed up and down the corridor behind her as she cocked her head this way and that to get a better perspective on things.

She tried to spot where it had happened. With her index finger she jabbed at various points on the map, intersections where streets crossed. Perhaps she would recognise the place when she came upon it.

In those days, ironically, there had been so much less motor-driven traffic to have to be careful about. What had got into her she had never been able to understand. Was it like vertigo, which (she'd read somewhere) is supposed to mask an unconscious wish to step off a high point and experience the elation and oblivion of plunging downward: or, like insomnia, which (she'd read somewhere else) is really the fear of falling asleep and discovering what thoroughly nasty and sordid imaginings you might conjure up in your dreams?

She'd walked off the edge of the pavement on to the road and in front of the car because ... Because ... Not because she'd guessed the man, *that* man, would reach out his arm and grab her and haul her back: she only knew him as a face — a handsome face — from the hotel, and it was only by chance that she'd turned and looked behind her a few seconds before the incident occurred and seen that he was there. Maybe it was because she'd disorientated herself slightly, turning her head on her shoulders to look round, that the episode had happened? Or could there have been deeper causes why she'd stepped on to the road at the very instant the car was rounding the corner? — the memory of Ranald Forbes waiting at home, in douce, sooty Glasgow, and the prospect of, first, the inevitable return to Scotland after their visit to Aunt Bessy in Menton and, then, the decision she would have to make before she saw Mrs Forbes and her elder son again. Perhaps her backward glance at the man — someone she'd noticed no more than half-a-dozen times and whom she knew nothing about — had disturbed her morning peace, and had prompted the thought of Ranald Forbes (never very far from her mind, but less insistent when she was walking in the sunshine): and the incident that followed had been set in motion by her subconscious acting?

Or the quality of light, could it have been? Had the sun been in her eyes on the crossing, and that was why she hadn't been able to see the car's hushed approach?

She'd been dazed for several seconds afterwards. Faces swam in front of hers, buildings teetered, the trees jigged. Then she'd focused, and it was the man she'd found she was looking at.

How solicitous he'd proved himself, how concerned everyone else — her family and their friends — had been for her. Concerned and also, she'd guessed, anxious and uneasy to know how it could have happened: as if suspecting that so terrible a thing couldn't have happened merely by chance, because how perilous then must every action in our lives become?

* * * *

Madame Lépront ran her eyes down her shopping list. One person required almost as much as two, that was the strange thing. Two people *could* live as cheaply as one, not that economy had ever been a consideration with them both.

Buying for one sometimes seemed a futile occupation. But she had her family to owe an obligation to, and she was Guy's widow, with all its responsibilities to his memory. There had been so much — there was still so much — which she should feel grateful to her late husband for having given her: even this very air to breathe.

* * * *

Without the incident happening, Miss Simm knew — the car turning the corner — the man wouldn't have had the excuse to see her as he was given permission to do afterwards. Otherwise her mother wouldn't have welcomed him to their table in the hotel dining-room of an evening, she wouldn't have allowed him to show them the lie of the coast and the rocky inland terrain as he did on half-a-dozen picnic expeditions. Frenchmen had always been untrustworthy on principle, but *he* was unconditionally exonerated of the faults of his race and granted a free pardon. If he hadn't had such excellent reflexes that he'd been able to shoot out his arm and tip her out of the car's path that day, she would most certainly not have found herself dining alone with a gallant foreign gentleman on a restaurant terrace strung with vines above a wild sea crashing on to boulders. In all probability she would have been maimed, or dead.

By the time she was meeting him alone, unchaperoned, her life seemed to have gone off at an improbable tangent, she was suddenly walking on an unlikely track, further and further from the landmarks she recognised. At twenty-two years old she wasn't quite prepared for it, nor for her second offer of marriage in a troubled season. In another year's time — who was to say? — perhaps she might have been.

Perhaps the car had turned the corner a year too soon?

* * * *

Madame Lépront glided silkily through the network of lanes that webbed the town. She felt cool in her washed-pink cotton shift. It billowed out behind her, in the fashionable style. She had good enough legs still to be able to go about with them bare. The espadrilles couldn't have been a better fit for her feet, and they might — in her current mid-morning frame of mind — have had wings.

Through her dark lenses she was aware that people were looking at her. She hoped they weren't playing the guessing-game about age: not that she was ashamed, but you *are* — the hoariest cliché in the book — as old or as young as you feel. Sometimes she felt rather less in command of herself, when the weather changed and the salt wind blowing inland over the rooftops seeped through the rubber seals on the windows and made twinges in her arms and shoulders and back. But that was only occasionally, and no one escapes scot-free.

A few people were in the habit of exchanging "good day" with her and she would drop a reply over her shoulder. She now passed as a native — and anyone would have been hard put to conclude that she was not. The language hadn't come easily to her, not until her first child was born, and then all the bits and pieces had seemed to fit into place. *"Ecossaise,"* she would reply if anyone did ever ask her where she was from originally, that rather than *"Anglaise"*: it left people much less certain about what to expect of her, and she preferred that her past should belong somewhere on the misty perimeter edge of their imagination. She chose to believe that every departure and new beginning in life is like a skin being shed: a character is compounding itself, and while the past is inevitably a part of it, it shouldn't be allowed to make falsely demanding claims. It doesn't — or shouldn't — ever *own* anyone.

* * * *

Miss Simm thought she had found the spot: then she wasn't so sure.

She couldn't quite get her directions. The names of the

streets on the signposts meant nothing to her. Payot, Péri, Cazin. After fifty years the country had a different set of heroes and liberators to commemorate. Avenue des Martyrs-de-la-Résistance, Avenue du Général de Gaulle, Boulevard Winston Churchill, Avenue des Commandos d'Afrique. She asked herself if they *could* possibly be the same plane trees in the square, if they weren't too sprightly to be the ones she'd walked under in 1936.

In those days the coast had also been a working one, and among the sights had been the schools of fishing boats chugging for the jetties after a day or night at sea. There were far fewer of the smacks now, only a handful. Of course there had been a *plage* then too, and flashy cars with running boards and white tyres, family groups like her own eating from picnic hampers, but the two ways of life — the indigenous and the elegantly fanciful — seemed to coexist in her mind. Now most of the town's business had to do with the wholesale pursuit of pleasure — and frankly she was disappointed. Shops were like stalls, their wares spilling on to the pavement so that it took all her concentration to keep herself from being directed by the pressure of bodies towards the kerb. People ate and drank as they walked about, just as they did at home. One or two of the cafés, with their customers fenced in from the drifting crowds, had something of the charm and style of those in Aix or Avignon. She could remember a restaurant along the coast — remember it just, the details — with a trellis or pergola and a vine overhead, and candles under glasses on the tables, and a trio walking between the tables playing she'd forgotten what on their violins, and a man talking to her: the words turning to ether as soon as he spoke them, his face only a couple of feet from hers but crossed with those shifting blue shadows.

* * * *

The past didn't *own* her, Madame Lépront knew. Nor was it an anchor. But her mind would play with it, turning it over as she turned over the curious debris of shells and sea life she found washed up by the tide on her beach-combing walks.

Thinking how, if she hadn't had an opportunity to meet Guy in the way she had, none of the rest would have happened. But how she might have had an opportunity to meet him at another time and place — and so the rest would still have happened, wouldn't it?

She was an optimist in these matters. If something is meant to occur, you may be given more than one chance, if you bungle the first. But it's up to you not to let it go a second time: fate has limited reserves of patience and doesn't tolerate fools, those who won't learn.

"My Robert the Bruce principle," she sometimes joked to those who would understand the parable of the spider and the watching king. Without it the Scots wouldn't have been the enterprising, persevering race she knew they were, and which she had proved by her own example.

* * * *

Conveniently, Miss Simm thought, I have presumed he must be dead — but what if he isn't?

She calculated. How old would he have been then, in 1936? Twenty-five or twenty-six, at least. Thirty at the outside. Add fifty to that.

It was perfectly possible that he *was* living: he was alive and well, walking along a promenade somewhere in white summer clothes, tanned and spry: his years of travelling here and there in the land business were behind him, but they'd left him handsomely provided for.

A bachelor? She'd stopped allowing for that possibility long ago, about the time she decided to call off her engagement to Ranald Forbes and watched Elspeth Colquhoun take her place. She had realised from people's shocked reactions in the two cities, Glasgow and Edinburgh (and also in such respectable havens as genteel Helensburgh and decorous Kilmacolm), that it was only the few hard-bitten cases who resisted the mating call, and that she'd chosen to do something quite unnatural.

He wouldn't have given up so easily, her Frenchman. On another evening in the same restaurant above the sea, the same scene would have repeated itself. She had imagined it so often. The girl who sits at the table listens to him and considers well as the trio coax such sweet music from their violins. The vine trellis maps an exactly similar grid of shadows, and this time the scene plays to its intended conclusion. The man smiles, so does the girl. His face and hands reach forward out of the blue shadows. The sea tumbles on the rocks far beneath them, its roar muted to polite, whispered sibilants. His companion smells lavender, a fragrance carried off the hills on the warm breath of the wind, and she dares to hope that all her life with the man will echo the happiness of these perfect moments.

* * * *

Madame Lépront walked downhill with long, confident strides. She wore dark glasses against the sun's glare.

The town spread beneath her, and beyond were the wooded slopes of Cap Bénat. She glanced at the promenade and the leafy square: gardeners were laying the dust, and the cafés had set out their wicker chairs and tables to lure customers.

The narrow back streets were the quickest way down and she was familiar with all the short cuts. Even after all her years in other cities she knew her way about like a local-born. Curiously, though, something about the place eluded her — a spirit — which she imagined she might have felt if she'd been living in, say, Antibes or St Jean-de-Luz. Maybe she hadn't been here long enough since her return to discover that sense of place, or was the town not quite big enough or old enough? The "spirit" had escaped her fifty years ago when she'd first arrived, when her eyes had been blinded by the sea light and she'd lived in a dizzy muddle: morning excursions in the car to what was judged worth seeing, evenings at the hotel enduring unending meals, lazy beach afternoons under sun umbrellas, expeditions across the sand-strewn streets to dark, cool shops and a café with a yellow awning that served green drinks and where a grinning man played an accordion accompaniment while a woman in a long nasturtium-coloured dress like a kimono sang slow, dirge-like songs that never seemed to have a melody.

* * * *

Now there were so many cafés and none of them had a yellow awning. Miss Simm searched but couldn't find it. Pop music seeped out of passing cars and floated down from upstairs rooms and wafted up from basements and she couldn't hear those tuneless songs any more that she used to listen to. The woman who sang them had had a painted face and most of the songs had been to do with Montparnasse and the *quartier* Saint-Germain. She used to wonder, why doesn't she go back to Paris if she's so homesick and spare us all? But the songs, their words and melodies forgotten now, had been woven into the woof of those oddly static, becalmed afternoons when she'd sat with her sister or brothers or cousins, sipping tea, watching the few cars pass, seeming — it occurred to her now — to be only waiting for something to happen to her.

* * * *

They'd lived in half-a-dozen places, and she'd come back to Le Lavandou. She wasn't sure why. It wasn't what it had been. Along the coast road there were still quieter spots, coves hidden by rocks and pines, and a couple of superior restaurants she sometimes went to, with terraces above the sea. Friends wrote or rang or visited from Paris and Geneva, and there was no risk of losing touch. (From longer ago there were still two cousins alive, ensconced in a Scottish spa town, but that was as much as she knew about them.) Children and grandchildren existed on the fringes of that mental map which composed her knowable world, in Switzerland and Belgium and America, and she believed herself distantly indispensable to them and never an intruder on privacy or a burden to conscience. At the centre of so much attention, she lived contentedly alone.

Maybe she'd meant coming back to Le Lavandou to be a drawing-in of all the threads? Here it had begun for her, one summer before the War, when she was another person: a silly accident-that-almost-was, stepping on to the road without looking first for traffic, and a hand — *his* hand, Guy's hand — reaching out for her. Now she was only paying her own

109

homage of sorts to that fleeting incident which had made her busy, practical, necessary life possible in the first place.

* * * *

Miss Simm wondered why she wasn't getting the "feel" of the streets. She had imagined that, somehow, instinct would guide her.

She was aware that people were looking at her, smiling in her face, but not for simple civility's sake.

She felt her tweeds were hanging heavily from her; the inside of her waist band was sodden with perspiration; her canvas shoes pinched.

She walked along the pavement however she could, jostled by arms and shoulders and hips. In *her* day there had been nothing like this: the people who'd come then, the cognoscenti had behaved with tact.

The proximity of so much unclothed flesh was alarming her. She smelt the sun oil: a brash, impertinent chemical odour that seemed first to fill her head, then to be weighing on it like a stone.

Suddenly she thought she couldn't trust her knees to hold her up any longer. She looked anxiously to either side of her before reaching out for the trunk of a plane tree to steady herself.

Her head was spinning. She blinked her eyes several times. With the tips of her fingers she stroked the silvery smooth bark. That at least was real, and confirmable, whether it was a tree from *then* — that long ago — or later.

It worried her that "then" could vanish with so little trace left behind: or, just as bad, that it could play these confusing tricks of identity, hiding up side streets where it knew she had no hope of finding it, changing its name and purpose and disguising itself behind smart, modern frontages and the swarms of smart, modern people.

Mystified, Miss Simm shook her head. Then, gingerly, she let go her fastness, the plane tree's trunk.

Screwing up her courage, she rejoined the tide of holiday-makers, and allowed herself to be carried along on the drift.

They moved more quickly than she or any of her friends were used to moving. Somehow, at a certain point in your life, you felt you should be spared the urgency to reach anywhere: what was coming to you would come, and whether you rushed there or not didn't make an iota of difference. But who would have understood that here, even if she'd been able to speak in their language?

The pavement burned through her shoes' thin soles. Her legs seemed to have hardly any strength left in them. If she'd heaped pebbles into her pockets — like Virginia Woolf in the biography from the library she'd once read — she couldn't have felt any more lethargic or doomed.

She stopped looking to her left or her right and gazed, blinkered, over the heads of those in front of her. She was still being stared at, she knew, by incredulous people trying to guess what had brought her here. Her Scottishness must be written all over her, her age must be a joke.

* * * *

Madame Lépront was remembering something else for her shopping list.

What was important was always to have an active mind. You couldn't keep age at bay, so why not accept it in a spirit of good grace, with a modicum of enthusiasm even? She'd known people who'd been middle-aged in their twenties, and people in their forties who'd seemed older than their parents.

It was all a matter of the mind's willingness, she was quite certain: a successful life answered to a positive, assertive attitude.

Attitude. Acknowledging the unlikeliness of failure was the best means of ensuring that failure was avoided.

Madame Lépront kept the spectres where they belonged, in the shadows. Far from Helensburgh and Kilmacolm, a thousand miles away, she walked in sunshine, in the widening, brightening glare of day.

* * * *

On the Place Reyer Miss Simm was thinking of Largs.

At home in the block of flats most of her neighbours were contemporaries: slow, creaking, stooped in their varying degrees. She and her friends took their daily constitutionals on the sea front where the wind blew briskly; they'd sold their real homes, their families had scattered far and wide, and what they had left was Largs, and each other, and the view across Gogo Water to Cumbrae and Bute and the peak of Goat Fell, and that other, much more intriguing prospect — the past.

As they walked to the Pencil at Bower Craig or to Barrfields or along the residential avenues, her group would watch with impatience their less able acquaintances shuffling and halting; one woman was always speeded past them in a wheelchair, as absurdly bright-cheeked as a baby in a pram.

They must be here in Le Lavandou too, Miss Simm thought, deposited in blocks of flats like filing cabinets — human retrieval systems — but discreetly removed from the biz, in some other part of the town.

As she walked on, willing one foot in front of the other, she felt she had escaped from elsewhere — that she was treading where she shouldn't, out of bounds now, that the middle-aged in their holiday undress were looking at her with the unkindest stares of all, as if she was a bearer of bad news.

Ridiculous, she told herself, I'm hallucinating: it's the heat's doing, and because I've found out there's nothing whatsoever to discover. I should never have left Largs. I'm a stay-at-home, I always was, Le Lavandou can't tell me anything I don't know already. That all was really for the best: that I decided according to the person I was, the one heredity made of me, because I was born to certain parents in a certain place far to the north of here at a certain point in the history of human affairs when a properly-reared young Scotswoman did not — most emphatically did *not* — lose her heart to an olive-skinned, dark-eyed Frenchman, however impeccably upright and principled and chivalrous she afterwards discovered his reputation to be.

* * * *

They'd lived well, she and Guy, to the full. The days had never been long enough for them, no sooner here than they were done. Like paper days being stripped off a calendar in films she'd seen. Their years together had flitted past, the allotted thirty-nine had been used up and she was left confused afterwards, unsure how she could have lived through so long a span and been so little conscious of its passing.

They'd balanced each other, she'd always felt. (Or did she mean "complemented"?) Guy had been resolute, unpersuadable once he was decided on something; but also fair, willing to understand a weakness in another and why it occurred; he'd had a tender and romantic side to his nature too, being so absurdly protective of her. Since Guy's death, she'd assumed those qualities to herself: the romantic impulse least successfully of all perhaps, because she'd been born a Scot but the kind who turns with age, not maudlin, but eminently practical and matter-of-fact.

Married to Guy, she'd felt she was one half of a whole: now she felt she was more than herself, she was one-and-a-half people, herself plus as much of Guy as she had managed to save.

He was with her, because so long as one of them was left, the other must be too, since they had been so close. She had no dealings with the widows — the handless kind or the guilty ones — who depended on their faith in mediums. A marriage was between two persons, and if mutual trust and confidence weren't there as a bond in the beginning they most definitely couldn't be learned in the hereafter.

* * * *

It was the tramping and slithering of feet Miss Simm heard on all sides of her, then — further off, so she imagined, but really only yards away and separating her from the palms and the promenade wall — the groaning and screeching of traffic, engines straining, brakes squealing, horns blaring. There was a smell of burning rubber, and she wondered how the trees survived so bravely and shiny-leafed after years in the suffocating, choking atmosphere of fumes.

She looked forward, over the heads in front of her, blinkered against the watching faces to left and right of her. She could ask, try to ask, but she didn't know what exactly it was she was looking to find. It was her feelings she was relying on to tell her, her instincts. Relying on, but she couldn't be sure . . .

Then, just seconds later, it seemed she had no doubts at all. She suddenly stopped in her tracks. She'd reached the end of the block. Turning her back to the shore and the sea, she looked up at the front of the building nearest her and saw with a start the word "Hôtel" in old-fashioned script, shining through the paintwork from another era.

People jostled around her, oiled limbs passed brazenly by, and she continued to look up. What had its name been? The Hôtel What?

She closed her eyes, trying to remember, trying to call it up, abracadabra it out of the past. A girl's name, wasn't it?

She opened her eyes slowly. She realised she was swaying on her feet. An arm reached out to steady her. Someone said something, in anxious-sounding French. She couldn't reply, not in kind, and she smiled as best she could.

"I think — I can manage, thank you," she said in a croaky voice, meaning to sound game, plucky.

She turned round. Ahead of her the building on the other side of the street was modern, it had too much glass. Or — her eyes widened — perhaps the glazed terraces on the ground and first floors were only recent additions, to what was much older.

She tilted her head further back to take in the rest of the building. One second it seemed as close as could be, the next it was as distant as what had happened years ago, or had not happened.

She tried to focus, to concentrate, but her eyelids wouldn't stay open. Her legs continued walking, but without any instruction from her that they should, no command at all. It was as if her limbs were another person's, or it was as if she was living in a stranger's body, she had been for years and only now did the ruse declare itself, at the very last moment.

Her legs carried her forward and there was no stopping them, nothing she could do even if she'd had the will. The traffic pulled and sucked like the tides, the people on all sides of her fixed her on her course, the pavement was like a channel running under her.

* * * *

But just ahead the pavement shelved and as she felt her legs start to give way beneath her she waited in that split second for a saving hand to reach out and grab her.

It didn't come.

Instead one side of her seemed to be blasted away with the impact, her right hand scorched on the metal.

Someone screamed. She heard, somewhere on the periphery of the moment, shouts.

Then she had the illusion of flying as Le Lavandou bore on her from every angle.

She was inside a kaleidoscope, she found, she was rattling round and round with the pieces, far from the sounds. Topsy-turvy, head-over-heels, round and round and round and round . . .

* * * *

In another part of the town Madame Lépront continued on her way, sublimely unaware of any mishap anywhere else.

Her shift blew behind her, her feet hardly touched the cobbles or paving stones in their haste to reach wherever it was they were taking her. She felt — even for her — unusually light and weightless.

She listened to the muffled roar of traffic beneath her in the crowded streets: revving cars, spluttering motorcycles, air brakes sighing on lorries, the tourist coaches sitting with their engines rumbling to keep the air-conditioning turning over.

Le Lavandou wasn't what it had been, but nowhere was: and it wasn't as it would be in another fifty years, nothing like.

She slowed as she walked downhill, towards the sea that gave the town its raison d'être. She removed her dark glasses and dropped them into her basket. Her eyes filled with bright crystalline light: it poured inside her head.

A breeze blowing uphill ruffled the folds of her fashionably pale pink shift around her knees.

A siren separated itself from the traffic noises and the squawking of seabirds overhead. She noticed an ambulance passing at the bottom of the street, with blue beacons flashing.

Momentarily her brow furrowed, but only for a moment — then the skin became smooth again and her expression cleared.

She carried on walking. Her shift blew out behind her. To anyone who might have seen, the breeze would have seemed to cut clean through her, just like a spirit.

Feather-light, as light as air, she passed on, unhurried and uncomplicated, like someone with only the livelong day to fill and not a thought in her head to hold her back.

* * * *

Then finally — in blissful, relieved slow motion and beyond pain — Miss Simm was diving

diving

diving

In her mind's eye she caught a last backwards glimpse of herself, reduced to just a speck, a particle.

Deeper and deeper, she was fathoms down in the silence, diving for oblivion and fade-out; disappearing into the cool blue wastes of all that annihilating summer sky.

DOUGLAS DUNN

Mozart's Clarinet Concerto

Andy Dunlop and Gub MacCluskey walked along Sidmouth
Street a few minutes after half-past five. "Who the hell was this
Sidmouth? Any idea?"

Gub MacCluskey persevered with his ritual of tobacco, paper
and fingers. He looked meditative, like a vet tending a small
mammal. "It's a place. Sidmouth's the name of a place," he said,
stretching the dark tobacco, "down south."

"Now y' mention it . . . It rings a bell. But how come we're
lumbered wi' it an' all then?"

"Don't give us that patter. How many streets are there
in this town? Any idea? Thousands, that's what. An' it's
no' all that big a country, is it? So it stands to reason,
Andy."

"Stands to what reason?" asked Andy Dunlop.

"There aren't enough names in Scotland to go round.
Places — fair enough, names galore. Streets — no way,
Andy. The planners 've just got to look elsewhere."

"I'll look that name up in the library." Despite the bell that
had rung a moment before, he was no longer convinced. "Mind
you, I'll admit it doesn't sound Scottish."

"Neither does Glasgow. It's only because y' know it is that y'
believe it is."

"I'm sure that's no' a wireless," said Andy Dunlop. They
listened. Their eyes roved from one storey of the tenement to
the next.

"Benny Craig," said Gub MacCluskey, snapping his fingers.
"That'll be who it is. The boy plays the clarinet."

"Davie Craig's boy?"

"Real serious boy, accordin' to Davie. If y' ask me, Davie's worried about that boy."

Staring up, with their faces screwed into pained expressions, they listened while a flock of starlings swept down on a ledge.

"What the hell kind of music *is* that?"

On the fourth floor, in a bedroom he shared with his two younger brothers, Ted Craig was practising with the devotion of a saint.

"Oh, I get it. Benny *Goodman*!"

"Play it, Benny!" Gub MacCluskey shouted through cupped hands held close to his mouth.

Ted Craig was preparing for an audition. His father still refused to believe he could force an entry on the Glasgow School of Music on the strength of a written test, an interview and a sample of his playing. "Y' haven't the qualifications, son. Y'll have to face up to the fact an' just accept it as a *hobby*."

"It's no' easy to tap y'r feet to *that*," said Andy Dunlop, whose right shoe was searching the pavement for a beat, smudging a heart drawn in chalk which advertised that two sets of initials were in love with each other.

"Aw, give over!" Gub MacCluskey shouted to the fourth-floor window. No one that high up could hear him. Ted was immersed in Mozart's *Clarinet Concerto*, the part where the clarinet enters for the first time and which — in case you've forgotten it — goes like this:

Ted Craig's mother opened the bedroom door. Television noises came in, and the sound of Ted's playing went out and was enough to make his brothers yell as if they were seriously pained. His eyes turned from his music which was propped against a pile of books on a sideboard. His fingers continued to play the next few bars from memory before he stopped. "A wee cup of tea, son?"

"How can I play this an' drink tea at the same time?"

"Y'r mouth'll get all dry playin' for as long as that."

Ted's father leaned from his armchair by the door until his head was visible. Hearing him clear his throat, Mrs Craig moved to one side. "You wet y'r whistle, son. I've told y', take it easy. If you've a big test comin', then keep somethin' in reserve."

Considerate, peace-making, Mrs Craig closed the door softly behind her and sat down again. "Can y' not turn that thing down a bit?" she said, knowing no one was likely to make a move towards the switch.

Once inside The Wheatsheaf, Gub MacCluskey and Andy Dunlop settled on their elbows before the bar. A man came over to them from the shadows. "Hear y'r all on strike boys," he said.

"Strike? No' us," they said to the small, middle-aged man.

"Oh . . . Oh, well, hell of a sorry, lads." The man backed off. "Awfully sorry. Sorry, boys." Timid confusion made his repeated statements of being sorry sound like condolences. "Hell of a sorry, lads . . ."

"Y' tell him y'r no' on strike, an' he apologizes? What's this world comin' to?" said Gub to Andy.

After a few words to some men who were sitting at a table in the darkness of the bar-room, the small man came back.

"They three there, *they* work at Passmore's, an' *they* say they're *definitely* on strike. *Official*," the man added, belligerently directing a finger several times at no one.

"Aye, sure, that's a fact."

"So?"

"So what? We work at MacCallum's."

"Oh . . . Oh, I *see*."

"Aye."

"Hell of a sorry to 've inconvenienced you men in that way." He backed off again. "Oh, God, aye, hell of a sorry."

The man returned to the table in the shadows.

"Who's he?" Andy Dunlop asked the barman.

"Him? Everybody calls 'im the Union Man."

"Union Man? Y' mean . . .? Y' mean, *he's* a union *organizer*?"

Touching the side of his head with a finger, the barman

said, "He wanted to be. Years ago, mind you. The man's no' aw there. He's a One Man Mental Workers' Resistance Movement."

Ted's father came in and sat on the edge of a bed. He motioned for Ted to keep playing. He was now working on the climactically arpeggiated ending of the first movement.

"Very good, son. It sounds a bit on the hard side."

"It's finger-music. It's aw below the fingers."

"Y'r comin' on, I'll say that. An' y'll no' have long to wait before y' find out what's what either. Y' got the wind up?"

"I don't fancy no' passin' it, if that's what y' mean."

"It wouldn't be the end o' the world, son. Quantity surveying's no' a bad line to fall back on."

"For somebody who wants to play this thing for a livin', it's about as bad as y' can get."

"Where you get y'r musical talent from'll always be a mystery to me. I canny even sing. Y'r mother's *never* been able to carry a tune."

"I've met that one before, Dad — canny be any good, his father canny even sing."

"Don't mind it too much when y'r playin' that man Mozart there. It's when y'r doin' these . . . *scales*. Jesus, son, it's like draggin' y'r teeth down a sheet o' sandpaper. Aye, well . . . I'm right behind y' now, Ted."

"What was it," said Ted, moved but unable to show it, "just a matter of time?"

"Not my time." His father looked at him. "It's the time *you've* spent playin' that thing. You know me, I'm useless at serious conversations." An embarrassed silence grew between them. "Just you play that, son. That's all. If you want to play that, then I take y'r point. You stick in. Wire in, son."

"Thanks, Dad," Ted said. "It'll make a difference, knowin' you don't think I'm wastin' time . . ."

"Play us that bit again," Davie Craig said, sitting back on the bed. "I'd like to hear that bit properly."

"What bit?"

"The bit y' were playin' when I came in. That bit wi' all these notes in it."

"Y' know," said Gub MacCluskey, putting his glass down,

"I'm in two minds if I'm right about Sidmouth bein' a place down south. You've confused me."

"It rings a bell, I'm tellin' y'. Right down, right down south somewhere. I think I saw somethin' about that place the year we were in Torquay."

"Torquay?"

"Aye, an' great digs there . . ."

"Sidmouth?" interrupted the Union Man, who was paying for a half-pint in coppers and doling them out one at a time into the barman's hand, knowing he didn't have enough, and knowing that the barman knew.

"Aye, Sidmouth," said Andy Dunlop, turning away from the stranger.

"Right bad man was Sidmouth," said the Union Man.

"It's a *place*. It's a *place*, down south." Gub MacCluskey made it clear he had had about enough of the Union Man.

"A big politico, a long time back . . . One o' the biggest reactionaries ever to cast a shadow on the workin'-man's movement." Each fatalistic emphasis added to Gub MacCluskey's increasing interest. "An' *that* was Sidmouth."

"Never knew anybody catch 'im out on matters of historical importance," said the barman. He rattled his handful of coppers. "Aye, an' another three pence, you."

"Are you sure about this?" asked Andy Dunlop.

"Sure I'm sure," said the small man.

As his price for finding out more, Andy Dunlop took three pence from the pile of coins beside his glass and gave them to the barman. "Awful good of you," said the Union Man, excessively polite. "An' I'm awfully sorry to 've intruded on y'r conversation like that, boys."

"We're no' finished wi' you yet," said Gub MacCluskey, catching the Union Man by the coat. "You tell us what y' know about this Sidmouth."

"Way back, in eighteen-twenty or eighteen-whatever-it-was . . . Strike isny the word for it. More like a rebellion. Soldiers in the streets. My mind's no' what it was, boys. I can't remember the way I used to."

"An this Sidmouth was one o' the swine that sent the troops in?"

"There was some poor radical-man hung, drawn, an' quartered because o' him. Dragged through the streets," said the Union Man, "on a cart, an' then hung an' cut up, in public. Down there, I'm tellin' y', in the Candleriggs."

He sidled away on his shuffling, short footsteps, looking after his half-pint which he held before him like a lamp.

"Don't know about you, but I'm writin' to the Lord Provost. Either they change the name o' that street or I'm takin' up terrorism."

"Take it easy," said Gub MacCluskey. "They're knockin' it down in six months anyway."

"Oh hello, Davie," said Andy Dunlop with more familiarity than Ted's father thought was called for. "We were just talkin' about y'r boy."

"Oh aye, which one?"

"Benny. We heard 'im earlier the night."

"Benny? I don't have a boy called 'Benny'."

"Oh."

"If it's Edward you mean," said Davie Craig, "then you call him that."

"Edward?"

"That's 'is name."

"Aye," said Gub MacCluskey. "Edward seems to be doin' well."

"I hear y'r on strike up at Passmore's," said Davie Craig.

"Och, no' again. We work at *MacCallum's*."

"Oh, sorry, boys."

"An' don't say that either. That's what *he* says."

"Who?" Davie Craig asked, following a nod towards where a small man sat hidden behind an opened second-hand newspaper.

"The Union Man."

"Poor soul," said Davie Craig. "He went on strike once too often."

Davie supped his beer. He began humming a tune. Gub MacCluskey and Andy Dunlop watched and listened. "The Mozart *Clarinet Concerto*," Davie explained. "Great wee tune, eh? I used to think that stuff was *rubbish*."

"*That's* what we heard 'im play," said Gub MacCluskey, snapping his fingers. He hummed the tune. "It's been on my mind, that." He hummed the tune and drummed his fingers on the wet bar. The Union Man lowered his paper to have a quick look at these three men who were humming the opening bars of the clarinet's solo in the first movement of Mozart's *Clarinet Concerto*.

"Oh, there's some lovely music been written," said Davie Craig. "*Lovely*. An' I haven't so much as bought my own boy a lesson. I didn't understand, y'see. But it's a great tune. It's a *great* tune. One of the all-time great melodies in my opinion."

Andy Dunlop and Gub MacCluskey nodded in agreement. Davie began humming the tune again. He was imagining his son sitting by the open bedroom window as his brothers slept, listening to Mozart's *Clarinet Concerto* rise from the city. His two companions joined in. They made gestures with their hands in time to the music. The Union Man looked over his newspaper again. "Oh, but it's a great tune," said Davie Craig. "An' the Slow Movement — the Slow Movement's *magic*." Davie closed his eyes. "While the Rondo — ah-ha, the Rondo *takes off*."

"Y' know about Sidmouth?" asked Andy Dunlop.

"Sidmouth?"

"*Lord* Sidmouth."

"Aye, I've heard about Lord Sidmouth. I've lived in that street," said Davie Craig, "all my married life."

"Does . . . eh, I mean, does y'r *boy*, Edward, y'r boy wi' the fancy ideas, does *he* know about Lord Sidmouth?"

"Oh, he knows. He knows all right. In more bloody ways than one. Hey, Union Man?" Davie shouted, to the newspaper that was cautiously lowered. "Do y' want a drink, Union Man?"

ALASDAIR GRAY

The New World

Millions of people lived in rooms joined by windowless corridors. The work which kept their world going (or seemed to, because they were taught that it did, and nobody can teach the exact truth) was done on machines in the rooms where they lived, and the machines rewarded them by telling them how much they earned. Big earners could borrow money which got them better rooms. The machines, the moneylending and most of the rooms belonged to three or four organisations. There was also a government and a method of choosing it which allowed everyone, every five years, to press a button marked STAY or CHANGE. This kept or altered the faces of their politicians. The politicians paid themselves for governing, and also drew incomes from the organisations which owned everything, but governing and owning were regarded as separate activities, so the personal links between them were dismissed as coincidences or accepted as inevitable. Yet many folk — even big earners in comfortable rooms — felt enclosed without knowing exactly what enclosed them. When the government announced that it now governed a wholly new world many people were greatly excited, because their history associated new worlds with freedom and wide spaces.

I imagine a man, not young or especially talented, but intelligent and hopeful, who pays for the privilege of emigrating to the new world. This costs nearly all he has, but in the new world he can win back four times as much in a few years if he works extra hard. He goes to a room full of people like himself. Eventually a door slides open and they filter down a passage to the interior of their transport. It resembles a small cinema. The emigrés sit watching a screen on which appears deep blackness spotted with little lights, the universe they are told they are travelling through. One of the lights grows so big that it is recognisable as a blue and white cloud-swept globe whose surface is mainly un-reflecting ocean, then all lights are extinguished and, without alarm, our man falls asleep. He has been told that a spell of unconsciousness will ease his arrival in the new world.

He wakens on his feet, facing a clerk across a counter. The clerk hands him a numbered disc, points to a corridor, and tells him to walk down it and wait outside a door with the same number. These instructions are easy to follow. Our man is so stupefied by his recent sleep that he walks a long way before remembering he is supposed to be in a new world. It is perhaps a different world, for the corridor is narrower than the corridors he is used to, and coloured matt brown instead of shiny green, but it has the same lack of windows. The only new thing he notices is a strong smell of fresh paint.

He walks very far before finding the door. A man of his own sort sits on a bench in front of it staring morosely at the floor between his shoes. He does not look up when our man sits beside him. A long time passes. Our man grows impatient. The corridor is so narrow that his knees are not much more than a foot from the door he faces. There is nothing to look at but brown paintwork. At length he murmurs sarcastically, "So this is our new world." His neighbour glances at him briefly with a quick little shake of the head. An equally long time passes before our man says, almost explosively, "They promised me more room! Where is it? Where is it?" The door opens, an empty metal trolley is pushed obliquely through and smashes hard into our man's legs. With a scream he staggers to his feet and hobbles backward away from the trolley, which is pushed by someone in a khaki dustcoat who is so big that his shoulders brush the walls on each side and also the ceiling: the low ceiling makes the trolley-pusher bend his head so far forward that our man, retreating sideways now and stammering words of pain and entreaty, stares up not at a face but at a bloated bald scalp. He cannot see if his pursuer is brutally herding him or merely pushing a trolley. In sheer panic our man is about to yell for help when a voice says, "What's happening here? Leave the man alone Henry!" and his hand is seized in a comforting grip. The pain in his legs vanishes at once, or is forgotten.

His hand is held by another man of his own type, but a sympathetic and competent one who is leading him away from the trolleyman. Our man, not yet recovered from a brutal assault of a kind he has only experienced in childhood, is childishly grateful for the pressure of the friendly hand. "I'm sure you were doing nothing wrong," says the stranger. "You were probably just complaining. Henry gets cross when he hears one of our sort complain. Class prejudice is the root of it. What were you complaining about? Lack of space, perhaps?"

Our man looks into the friendly, guileless face beside him and, after a moment, nods: which may be the worst mistake of his life, but for a while he does not notice this. The comforting handclasp, the increasing distance from Henry who falls further behind with each brisk step they take, is accompanied by a feeling that the corridors are becoming spacious, the walls further apart, the ceiling higher. His companion also seems larger and for a while this too is a comfort, a return to the safety of childhood when he was protected by bigger people who liked him. But he is shrinking, and the smaller he gets the more desperately he clutches the hand which is reducing his human stature. At last, when his arm is dragged so straight above his head that in another moment it will swing him clear of the floor, his companion releases him, smiles down at him, wags a kindly forefinger and says, "Now you have all the space you need. But remember, God is trapped in you! He will not let you rest until you amount to more than this."

The stranger goes through a door, closing it carefully after him. Our man stares up at the knob on it which is now and forever out of his reach.

JANICE GALLOWAY

Paternal Advice

(Scenes from the Life: No. 23)

It is a small room but quite cheery. There is an old-style armchair off to the left with floral stretch covers and a shiny flap of mismatching material for a cushion. Behind that, a dark fold-down table, folded down. On the left, a low table surmounted by a glass bowl cut in jaggy shapes, containing keys, fuses, one green apple and some buttons. Between these two is an orange rug and the fireplace. The fireplace is the focal point of the room. It has a wide surround of sand-coloured tiles and a prominent mantelpiece on which are displayed a china figurine, a small stag's head in brass, a football trophy and a very ornate, heavy wrought-metal clock. On the lower part of the surround are a poker and tongs with thistle tops and a matchbox. Right at the edge, a folded copy of the *Sunday Post* with the Broons visible on top. Behind the fireguard, the coals smoke with dross. The whole has the effect of calm and thoughtfulness. It is getting dark.

Place within this, the man SAMMY. He is perched on the edge of the armchair with his knees spread apart and his weight forward, one elbow on each knee for balance. He sits for some time, fists pressing at his mouth as he rocks gently back and forth, back and forth. We can only just hear the sound of a radio from next door, and the odd muffled thump on the wall. More noticeable than either of these is the heavy tick of the clock.

SAMMY exhales noisily. He appears to be mulling over some tricky problem. He is. But we are growing restless in the silence.

Suddenly, too close, a noise like a radio tuning and we are in the thick of it.

> put it off long enough and it wasnt doing the boy any favours   just kidology to make out it was   just putting it off for himself more like   no   time to face it and get on with it right   it was for the best after all and a father had to do his best by his boy even if it was hard even if he didnt want to   bad father that shirked his responsibilities no bloody use to anybody   the boy had to be learned right and learned right right from the word go   right   spare the rod cruel to be nobodys fool that sort of thing right christ tell us something we dont know

The man stands up abruptly, scowling.

> no argument it needed doing   just playing myself here its HOW thats the thing thats the whole bloody thing is HOW   needed to be sure about these things tricky things needed to be clear in your mind before you opened your mouth else just make an arse of the whole jingbang just fuck it up totally TOTALLY aye got to be careful only one go at it right had to get it across in a oner and he had to learn it get the message right first time right had to know what you were at every word every move or else

SAMMY walks briskly to the window in obvious emotional agitation, bringing a dout from his right trouser pocket, then a box of matches. He inserts the dout off centre between his lips, takes a match from the box, feels for the rough side and sparks the match blind. The cigarette stump lights in three very quick, short puffs and still his eyes are focused on something we cannot see, outside the window in the middle distance. Up on tiptoes next, peering. Violent puffing. He shouts. BASTARDS! SPIKY-HEIDED BASTARDS. AD GIE THEM PUNK. WHAT DO THEY THINK THEY LOOK LIKE EH? JUST WHAT DO THEY THINK THEYRE AT EH? and he is stubbing the cigarette butt out on the sill, turning sharply, going back to the easy chair to resume his perch. He runs one hand grease-quick through his hair from forehead to the nape of his neck and taps his foot nervously.

christs sake get a grip eh remember what youre supposed to be doing eh   one thing at a time   TIME the time must be getting on. Get on with it. Hardly see the time now dark already. Right. Thats it then. That does it. Wee Sammy will be wondering what the hell is going on what his daddy is doing all this time

SAMMY's eyes mist with sudden tears as the object of his sentimental contemplation appears in an oval clearing above the man's head. A thinks balloon. Inside, a small boy of about five or six years. He has ash-brown hair, needing cut, a thick fringe hanging into watery eyes that are rimmed pink as though from lack of sleep. It is WEE SAMMY. The balloon expands. WEE SAMMY in a smutty school shirt, open one button at the neck for better fit, and showing a tidemark ingrained on the inside. One cuff is frayed. The trousers are too big and are held up by a plastic snakebelt; badly hemmed over his sandshoes and saggy at the arse. He is slumped against the wall of what we presume to be the lobby. It is understandable his father is upset to think of him: he looks hellish. God knows how long the boy has been waiting there. The eyes, indeed the whole cast of the body suggest it may have been days. And still he waits as we watch.

SAMMY clenches his eyes and the balloon vision pops. POP. Little lines radiate into the air to demonstrate with the word GONE in the middle, hazily. Then it melts too. The man makes a fist in his pocket but he speaks evenly. RIGHT. MAKE YOUR BLOODY MIND UP TIME. RIGHT. Then he springs to the door where he steadies himself, smooths his hair back with the palm of a hand and turns the doorknob gently. A barless A of light noses in from the lobby with an elongated shadow of the boy inside. The man's face is taut, struggling to remember a smile shape. One hand still rests on the doorknob, the other that brushed back his hair reaches forward, an upturned cup, to the child outside. A gesture of encouragement.

SAMMY: Come away in son.

The shadow shortens and the child enters, refocussing in the dim interior. The door clicks as his father closes it behind him and the boy looks quickly over his shoulder. The man smiles more naturally now as if relaxing, and settles one hand awkwardly on the boy as they walk to the fireplace. Here, the man bobs down on his hunkers so his eyes are more at a level with his son's. WEE SAMMY's eyes are bland. He suspects nothing. The man has seen this too and throughout the exchange to come, is careful: his manner is craftedly diffident, suffused with stifled anguish and an edge of genuine affection.

(pause)

SAMMY: Well. Youre getting to be the big man now eh? Did your mammy say anything to you about me wanting to see you? About what it was about?

WEE SAMMY: (silence)

SAMMY: Naw. Did she no, son? Eh. Well. Its to do with you getting so big now, starting at the school and that. You like the school?

WEE SAMMY: (silence)

SAMMY: Daft question eh? I didnt like it much either son. Bit of a waster, your da. Sorry now, all right. They said to me at the time I would be, telled me for my own good and I didnt listen. Youll see they said. Thought they were talkin rubbish. What did I know eh? Nothin. Sum total, nothin. Too late though! Ach, were all the same. Anyway, whats this your das trying to say, youll be thinkin. Eh. Whats he saying to me. Am I right?

130

WEE SAMMY: (silence)

SAMMY: Why doesnt he get on with it, is that what youre thinkin eh? Well this is me gettin on with it as fast as I can son. Its somethin I have to explain to you. Because Im your daddy and because youre at the school an everythin. Makin your own way with new people. Fightin your own battles. Im tryin to make sure I do it right son. Its like I was saying about the school as well, about tellin you somethin for your own good. But Im hopin youll be like me, that youll listen right. And thats why Im tellin you now. Now youre the big man but no too big to tell your old daddy hes daft. Eh wee man?

SAMMY rumples his sons hair proudly. WEE SAMMY smiles. This response has an instantly calming effect on the man and he raises himself up to his full height again. His voice needs to expand now to reach down to the boy. His demeanour is altogether more assured and confident.

SAMMY: OK. Thats the boy. Ready? One two three go.

WEE SAMMY remains silent but nods up smiling at his father as SAMMY pushes his hands under the boys oxters and lifts him up to near eye-level with himself.

SAMMY: Up up you come. Hooa! Nearly too heavy for me now. Youre the big fella right enough! Now. Heres a seat for you. No be a minute, then up on your feet.

He places his son on the mantelpiece between the brass ornament and the clock. He shifts the clock away to the low table, pats some stooriness off the shelf with the flat of his hand, then lifts the boy high, arms at full stretch, to reposition him in the centre of the mantelpiece in place of the clock. The boy is fully upright on the mantelpiece.

SAMMY: Upsadaisy! Up we go!

WEE SAMMY: Dad!

SAMMY: What? What is it son? Not to take my hands away? Och silly! Youre fine. On you come, stand up right, straighten your legs. Would I let you fall? Eh? Thats my wee man, thats it. See? Higher than me now, nearly up to the ceiling. OK? Now, are you listening to me? Listen hard. I want you to do somethin for me. Will you do somethin for me? Will ye son? Show me youre no feart to jump eh? Jump. Jump down and Ill catch you.

There is a long pause. The man is staring intently into the child's eyes and the child's eyes search back. He is still tall on the mantelpiece among the china and brass ornaments, back and hand flat against the wallpaper flora. The man's eyes shine.

SAMMY: Show your daddy youre no feart son. I'll catch you. Dont be feart, this is your da talkin to you. Come on. For me. Jump and I'll catch you. Dont be scared. Sammy, son, I'm waiting. I'm ready.

A few more seconds of tense silence click out of the clock. WEE SAMMY blinks. His hands lift from the wall and he decides: one breath and he throws himself from the screaming height of the sill. In the same second, SAMMY skirts to the side. The boy crashes lumpily into the tiles of the fire surround. His father sighs and averts his eyes.

SAMMY: Let that be a lesson to you son. Trust nae cunt.

LIZ LOCHHEAD

Phyllis Marlowe:
Only Diamonds Are Forever

The letters lying there on the mat didn't exactly look as though if I didn't open them the world would stop.

I picked them up. I turned them over, squinting through the bloodshot marblings of my hangover and the tangled remains of last night's Twiggy eyelashes. It was back in sixty-six. Those days the world was a more innocent place.

I fanned out the fistful of manilla in my mitt. As I had thought. Zilch. A final demand from the Gas Board and a threat from Glasgow Public Libraries if I didn't return *The Maltese Falcon* and pay my seventeen-and-six fine they'd permanently withdraw my ticket and cut my left hand off. And what was this? I swallowed. I swallowed again. An appointment card, report today, today at two-thirty, the Brook Clinic, a discreet logo and address, a classy address in the city's ritzy West End.

I showered, shaved — shaved my legs — like I said this was back in sixty-six, the world was a more innocent place, those days no one accused you of anti-feminism if you were caught with a tube of Immac. I sniffed. I showered again.

I emerged from the bathroom a half an hour later in a cloud of Amplex Aerosol avalanched in Boots' 365 Talcum. The place looked like the ski-slopes at Chamonix.

I shimmied shivering to the bedsit, slotted another shilling in the gas fire and reached for the knob on the third drawer of the tallboy. I knew exactly what I was looking for, they had to be here somewhere, the one and only pair of knickers left uncontaminated in that disastrous load at the launderette, the stuff that had got washed along with that bargain-price

133

bright-pink non-fast Indian-cotton mini-skirt from C&A. Some bargain, huh? These days I peeked out at the world through unevenly rose-tinted underwear.

I found them at last. Virgin white as the day they crossed the counter at Galls. I slid them on. Two-thirty, huh? I showered again.

Two-twenty-five found me on the steps of a slightly crumbling mansion in what the Estate Agents would call a highly desirable residential area. A simple brass plaque spelt out Brook Advisory Clinic. The whole place screamed Anonymity.

I pressed the bell. The door creaked open a couple of inches.

"Yes?" said a voice more frosted than its glass panels. I showed her my card.

"Two-thirty," I barked.

She barked back, the door slid open wide enough for me to enter and I found myself in a roomful of dames all with rigor mortis of the third-finger-of-the-left-hand. Engagement rings. Woolworth's engagement rings, each a lump of glass as big as the Ritz. There was more imitation ice than in *The Ancient Mariner,* more gilt than in a psychiatrist's office, more rolled gold than in Acapulco.

Tonight these dames were going to have greener fingers than Percy Thrower.

Each broad had a Tame Boyfriend with her, like a poodle on a lead. All you could see of any of them was a pair of very pink ears sticking out behind old copies of the *Woman's Own.* Nobody in the place looked exactly relaxed.

I sat down. Dame opposite was wearing laddered black Beatle nylons — Jesus, nobody had worn Beatle nylons since sixty-four Chrissakes. She was reading *The Uses of Literacy.* Maybe she did have an honours degree in sociology, but she certainly was sixpence short in the shilling when it came to dress-sense. Still, somebody loved her. Otherwise she wouldn't be here. I slid my eyes over the gent she had accessorising her. Below magazine-level at any rate he was not painful to look at.

Over in the corner behind a gigantic desk sat this old bird who looked as though she had been there since Marie Stopes was pre-pubescent.

"Next!" she plainsonged and fixed me with an old-fashioned look from behind her lorgnette.

I sidled over. "Name," she stated.

"Marlowe," I quipped. "Marlowe with an 'e'. Phyllis Marlowe. 'Ph' for Phellatio, 'Y' for Yesplease, 'L' for Love, 'L' for Leather, 'I' for Intercourse, 'S' for —"

She looked at me as though I had said a dirty word.

"In here," she said, "remove tights and pants, lie up on that table. Doctor will be here to examine you directly." She pronounced it Doktor with a "k". I gulped. I must pull myself together. I loosened my waistband and pulled myself together.

I found myself in a rough cubicle with a torn curtain hanging to approximately knee-height. Through this, various bits of anonymous female gooseflesh and, in the ringing tones of a Roedean Gymmistress, Doktor's voice interrogating the bimbo-next-door about the ins-and-outs of her sexlife. The whole place was about as private as Grand Central Station on Glasgow Fair Saturday.

Five minutes later found me flinching and clenching, biting into the black vinyl of the couch as cold steel penetrated. I spat out a curse.

Ten minutes after that — I sat in triumph, six precious months supply of the pill in my grasp.

Doktor wagged a metronome finger at me.

"You must take for twenty-one days religiously, stop for seven, always begin on the same day of the week, got it? Now, what do you do?"

"I'm a student at Jordanhill college doing Fribble," I riposted.

She gave me a look, I returned it, she slammed it back, I caught it neatly, spun round and delivered a deft backward glance over my left shoulder.

Back in the waiting room it had gotten twice as crowded. Obviously there was a future in this business, they'd hit a nerve somewhere.

Then I saw him. Shoulder-length blond hair, embroidered cheese-cloth shirt, single strand of beads — I mean, beads but *tasteful* — a sensual hint of hash and patchouli, and midnight blue denims stretched taut then flaring over the longest, leanest bass-guitarist's thighs in Glasgow. Like, this guy's loons had *style*. I'd loved him for as long as I could remember. I'd have known him anywhere.

"Haw, thingmy," he jack-knifed to his feet. "Whit urr you daeing here?"

"I might ask you the same question."

His Adam's apple slid up and down his throat like the lift in the Red Road Flats oughta, but don't.

"Hey, listen doll, great to see you, oh aye. Hiv tae git you roon tae wir new flat in Wilton Street, listen to a few albums, smoke a few joints. Fat Freddy's got some Moroccan in, really good stuff . . . toodle-oo!" he gabbled.

I looked over his shoulder. Coming towards him, big smile freezing fast, was this Julie Christie lookalike in Fringed Suede.

I smiled a lopsided smile. "So long Blue-Eyes, see you around."

Outside it was still raining. On my way through Kelvingrove Park I flipped my once-precious packet into a wastebasket and walked on.

Last I saw, a couple of hand-in-hand schoolkids had fished them out and were avidly reading the instruction leaflet. Probably disappointed to find it wasn't twenty-one tabs of acid. Sex is wasted on the young.

Back in my bedsit, I spooned bitter instant into my Union-Jack-I'm-Backing-Britain mug — this was sixty-six, the world was a more innocent place — and sighed. I guessed I'd just have to swallow it strong and hot and black and bitter, I'd run clean out of Marvel. I ripped the cellophane off another packet of chocolate digestives.

MAUREEN MONAGHAN

Saturday Song

He was about fourteen, clean, tidy and unlovely. Some sort of
skin complaint, he was told; you'll grow out of it soon, he was
promised. Meanwhile, he kept his boiled-looking face as much
to himself as possible, and when he rubbed and scratched the
raw cracks in his hands under the school desk, the teacher
asked him what he was fidgeting with, and the other boys
sniggered. Apart from scratching his hands, he seldom made
any superfluous movements. So he was not kicking stones or
crushing handfuls of the dusty hedge on that bright October
morning. He just sat quietly on a low wall, clutching a small
case and a cheap plastic folder under his arm. The wall faced
the back of a row of crumbling houses, and the boy was staring
absently at a broken window in the second house from the end.

An old man came slowly along the lane and into the yard.
When he saw the boy, he stiffened, straightened his back and
gathered his bulging string shopping bags close to him.

"What do you want?" He sounded weary. There was no
answer. "I said, what d'you want?" There was fear in the old
man's voice.

There was a pause, then the boy said, "Nothing. I'm just
waiting."

"Well you can't wait here. On your way, laddie!"

"No. I'll just stay. It's too early to go yet. I won't get in your
way." The boy spoke politely.

The old man almost mustered a roar, "Move, son! I
suppose it was your lot done that! Just get out of here
and leave me in peace. Away home and break your own
windows!"

"I'm sorry about your window," said the boy, "but I've just got here." He stood up.

"I'm only waiting for a while, but I'll move along there if you like."

He turned towards the old man, towards the other end of the shabby terrace, his mild blue eyes blinking and watering in the sun. There was no menace in him after all, no anger, except in the red blotchy skin. The old man sagged, too tired to argue any more. He handed over his bags and his keys as if to a neighbour of long standing. "Will you carry the messages in for me, lad? They're heavier than I thought."

The door opened into a narrow, stone-floored hallway smelly with paraffin cans, old newspapers and the passing attentions of cats. The boy had to squeeze himself against flaking, grey distemper to let the old man pass him and open the door half-way along the hall. A new set of smells and the twittering of a budgie greeted them as they entered the living-room.

The boy almost retched as the combined odours of birdcage, bed and old age reached him. The old man, unnoticing, said, "Come in, son. This is where I live. It's not very grand, but it does me fine. Could you put some coal on? It's a bit cold."

He sank into a worn, lumpy armchair. The boy put the string bags on the table and laid down his own case and folder too. He looked around for tongs or a shovel, then used his hands, reluctantly.

"Who's C.P.M.?"

The boy turned, startled. The old man was looking at the case. "Oh, that was my Dad, Colin Peter Morrison. I'm just Peter."

"Your Dad's passed on, then? What's in the case?"

"Nothing. A clarinet. It was my Dad's."

The old man looked eager. "Can you play it?"

"No!"

"Not even a wee bit?"

"No. I hate it!"

"Are you learning to play it?"

"No. My Mum sent me to lessons. But I hate it. Can I wash my hands?"

"Over there. Why d'you hate it?"

But Peter turned on the tap and washed his hands carefully. Then since the water was hot, he wiped out the greasy sink and started to wash the dishes which were in the sink, beside the sink, on the table and on the mantelpiece. He wet an old cloth which was bundled on the wooden draining-board, and washed off the ash and coal-dust and tea stains from the hearth. He looked at the filthy cloth.

"I think I should just throw this away now."

"Aye! You're a tidy fellow. D'you like the bird? Her name's Jinty. She's good company."

"Uh-huh. My Dad used to keep birds, but my Mum never liked them. I could clean out the cage. Does she get out?"

"She'll not go far. She likes the mantelpiece."

Peter opened the cage door with the bird trying to peck his fingers. It fluttered on to the old man's head, flew over to one of the square, varnished bedposts and finally settled on the brightly painted toffee-tin above the fireplace, squawking quietly.

The old man said soothingly, "Sssh, beauty, ssh! He's just making your house nice. He'll not hurt you."

Peter crossed to the sink to fill the little water bowl. "Where d'you keep the birdseed?"

"Here, I've just bought some more. She'll soon get used to you." He hesitated, then added, "She'll know you next time."

"Mr Briggs, could I . . .?"

"How d'you know my name?" the old man asked sharply.

"Your pension book. It's on the mantelpiece. It's just a different colour from my Mum's."

"Don't miss much, do you son?" he mumbled.

"Mr Briggs, I could come for a while on Saturdays, and . . . and help you. You know, clean up a bit, or go to the shops. I haven't . . . I mean there's nothing else to do." Peter held his finger out to the budgie. The bird ignored him, flew back to the cage and warbled at its reflection in the tiny mirror. "Would you like me to wash the window? I've still got time."

"Leave it, lad. You can do it next week."

Peter shut the door of the birdcage. "Oh! Fine! I'll come about ten."

"That'll be nice." The old man's gaze was resting on the clarinet case. "Why d'you hate it?"

"What? Oh! I just do."

"Play us a tune."

"No! I've told you! I can't. I'll need to go now." The red patches glowed on Peter's face and neck.

"What were you waiting for, son?"

"Nothing. It doesn't matter." Behind his back he rubbed his itching hands against his trousers, against each other. "Will I come next Saturday then?"

He tucked the clarinet and the folder under his arm. The old man was running his thumb-nail back and forward over the top of the birdcage. "What d'you think, Jinty? Will we let him come back? Maybe he'll give us a tune next time."

The bird cocked its head, first to one side, then to the other. Peter opened the door into the damp hallway.

"Jinty says you can come. You could wait at the end of the lane and carry the messages. If you want to."

Peter's fiery skin began to cool. "Right! Cheerio! See you on Saturday, Mr Briggs."

"Shut the doors behind you, son!"

Peter shut the living-room door. Going down the hall, he added shyly, "Cheerio, Jinty."

Their Saturday mornings settled into an easy routine. Peter, always with the clarinet and music-folder under his arm, would meet Mr Briggs outside the corner shop. The old man would hand over his bags and they would walk slowly, companionably, along the lane which became barer and muddier as the weeks went on. Once inside the house, the boy would fill the coal buckets while the old man made tea. They would drink it in front of the fire and slip cake crumbs to the budgie through the bars of the cage. Then Peter would gather up everything that looked like rubbish, take it out to the dustbin and push an ancient, rattling sweeper over the thin carpet. He would clean out the birdcage, and wash the window, if it wasn't raining. Mr

140

Briggs would potter around, put away his meagre groceries, start to peel potatoes, then abandon them in favour of another mug of stewed tea.

The conversation was hardly more varied than the housework.

"And how's the school, lad?"

"Fine."

"Doing all right then?"

"Uh-huh."

"You mind and stick in. I wish I had."

"Uh-huh."

Peter would brace himself for the next bit.

"How about a wee tune, then? Me and Jinty would like a wee tune. Wouldn't we, beauty?" The bird would trill obligingly.

Sometimes the old man held out the clarinet case towards the boy. Sometimes he would open it and stroke the red plush lining, or run his finger along the dark, shiny wood. "C'mon son. Play us a tune."

"No! I can't."

"Aw, you could if you tried."

"I don't want to!"

Mr Briggs would shake his head, sigh loudly and return to his potato peeling, looking hurt. Eventually he would say, "Is there time for more tea?"

And Peter would look at his watch, pick up his things and say, "No. I'd better be going. Will I come again next week?"

They would both look round the hot, tidy room.

"Aye, laddie. See you next Saturday."

The last Saturday in November was wild and stormy. Peter was already soaked by the time Mr Briggs came out of the shop with his usual string bags tucked inside plastic carriers. They ploughed along the filthy lane, heads down against the rain, bumping into each other as they fought the wind. The old man kept tugging at his hat and pulling up his coat collar, but Peter had the shopping in one hand and the clarinet and music-case in the other, and the rain dribbled unchecked round his neck and wrists.

"It's a dirty day, all right," said Mr Briggs, sounding quite cheerful. "I wondered if you'd bother coming."

"I said I would." The carrier-bags cut into Peter's hand, and he thought he might drop something.

"You're a good lad. We'll soon be home. The fire should be just nice when we get in."

They turned into the yard and the wind blew the bags against Peter's wet legs as he struggled across the path to the door. When the door was opened, Peter almost fell into the hallway. He hurried into the stuffy, fetid living-room and dropped everything in a heap on the table. His hands were aching with cold, and he stood about miserably while Mr Briggs hung up his coat and hat, and filled the kettle.

"Get that wet jacket off you, son. You'll maybe have to stay a bit longer, till it dries. I'll make the tea. You sit and warm yourself."

Peter took off his anorak and bundled it over the back of a chair. The old man had poked the fire and put pieces of coal round it without spoiling its blazing heart. Peter held out his hands to it, knowing that he should have rubbed his dripping hair and patted the wet cracks between his fingers. Already he could feel his face becoming taut in the dry heat. He crossed to the sink, let the water run for a minute, then put the stopper in. "I'd better get busy. There's a lot to do."

Mr Briggs reached from behind him and turned off the tap. "Nothing that won't wait, laddie. Come away from there. Just sit down, like I said, and get this tea inside you."

Peter sat in one of the fireside chairs with his hands wrapped round the steaming mug. Mr Briggs brought a plate of sticky buns and put it on the hearth near the boy.

"Mind and save some bits for Jinty. I'll let her out for a wee flutter." He opened the cage, but the bird remained on its perch, singing ecstatically. He looked at the budgie fondly.

"She likes it when it's raining. She knows fine we'll not rush off and leave her."

He held out a piece of his bun into the cage. The bird pecked it out of his fingers, dropped it and went on singing. "Cheeky thing!" he said indulgently.

Peter started to drink his tea. His face was burning, and between mouthfuls of tea and bun he hunched up first one shoulder, then the other, and rubbed the flaming patches on his cheeks against his rough sweater.

"What's wrong, lad?"

"Nothing."

"You don't look right. What's wrong with your face?"

"Nothing!"

Before the old man could ask any more questions, the bird flew out of the cage and rested for a moment on Peter's head on its way to the mantelpiece. The old man was delighted. "Oh, I knew she'd get used to you! She likes you! You'll not get rid of her next week!"

"I won't be here next week," said Peter quietly.

"What? Why not?"

"I can't come. I won't be coming again. I'll just tidy up a bit now. Maybe during the holidays . . ." he said half-heartedly, while rubbing his itching hands on his trousers. He brought the carpet-sweeper out from the cupboard in the wall and pushed it around the middle of the room. Mr Briggs kept getting in the way.

"Why can't you come? Why did you come in the first place?"

"It doesn't matter."

Peter left the sweeper standing, took a duster from under the sink and swept it smartly along the mantelpiece. The startled bird swooped round the room three times before heading for the cage. Peter's hand reached the cage door first.

"No you don't! I'm going to clean your cage properly — and you keep it clean!"

The bird sat on top of the cage looking puzzled.

"Just leave it, son. She's tired. Leave it till next week."

143

"I told you! I won't be back!"

"You haven't told me much. Why are you here?"

Peter ignored him. "I'll just give her clean water," he said, taking the plastic bowl to the tap. The bird scrambled into the cage, and the boy replaced the bowl and shut the door.

"You should be up at the school, shouldn't you?" The old man was jubilant when he saw the change in Peter's face. "Shouldn't you?"

"No!"

"I heard about those music lessons. Trumpets and flutes and violins. All sorts of things. And clarinets!" he added triumphantly.

"I don't have to go!"

"Aye, but that's where your Ma thinks you've gone! Isn't it?" He lifted the clarinet case from the table and thrust it under Peter's nose. The boy turned his head away.

"What happened son? Why can't you come next week? Did someone tell on you?"

"No! But I can't come back."

Peter busied himself at the sink. He thought of all the excuses he had already given his music teacher. He thought of all the other excuses he had stored up ready, but which he could not now use because his music teacher had stopped believing him. At least he could blame the weather this week. He heard Mr Briggs opening the catches of the case and waited for the dreaded wheedling words.

"We'll surely get a tune this time, Jinty. He couldn't leave us without a tune!"

Peter clashed the dishes in the soapy water. He pulled out the stopper and piled them on the draining-board.

"C'mon son. You know how much we want to hear you play! We don't mind if you're not very good!"

Peter half-dried his sore, raw hands. He took his anorak from the chair near the fire and put it on. It steamed with his body's heat. He started to tidy the bags he had dumped on the table, first laying his music-folder on one side.

"Maybe he can't play at all, Jinty! Maybe he just carries that case because it looks nice! If he doesn't play us a tune this time, we'll never know, will we?"

The itch between Peter's fingers was unbearable. He rushed the sweeper across the room and jammed it into a corner. "All right! All right!"

He snatched the case from the old man's hands and banged it down on the table. Deftly, he screwed the sections of the clarinet together, lining up the keys as if it was the habit of a lifetime. He took the protective metal cap off the mouthpiece, sucked the reed before positioning it and tightened the silver ligature which kept it in place. Mr Briggs was fascinated by the busy, skilful hands. He only noticed the boy's grim face when it glared redly a few inches from his own. He shrank back into his armchair.

Peter hissed at him, "I'll give you a tune! And your stupid bird as well! You've asked for it. You'll be sorry. Here's a tune for you!"

He stuck the clarinet angrily in his mouth and blasted hard, crude notes at the old man, repeating the vulgar theme over and over like a cruel, taunting child.

Hands to his ears, Mr Briggs whimpered, "Stop it! Oh, stop it, lad! It doesn't matter about the tune. You're frightening the bird!"

The terrified budgie was screeching and flapping, banging itself off the sides of the cage, scattering birdseed and water and tiny green feathers through the bars. Peter turned away from the old man. He blew long, unpitched rasps towards the bird, holding the clarinet in one hand while he opened the cage door with the other. He pushed the bell of the instrument into the cage, crouching level with the table on which it stood. The little quivering creature scrambled dementedly between floor and perch. It puffed out its heaving breast as if to push away the vicious, insistent tune. Mr Briggs stumbled over from his chair and pummelled Peter with his old soft fists, pleading and sobbing.

The bird was suddenly calm. It chirped once, and keeled over on its side at the bottom of the cage, one tiny eye staring beadily

145

upwards. It gave a gentle shudder, then lay still. Peter stared in horror at the dead bird.

The old man wailed, "You've killed her! You wee bugger! You wicked wee bugger! You've killed Jinty! Oh, the poor bird! You've killed her!"

The boy pulled the clarinet roughly out of the cage and ran out of the room and down the hallway, with the cries ringing in his ears. He ran across the yard and along the lane, ran all the way home in the driving, sleety rain. At last he stood, dripping and panting, on his doorstep and fumbled for his key. At some point he must have put the instrument inside his anorak for protection, and he realized, as his fingers touched the clammy wood, that he had left the clarinet-case behind.

The wind had died and the rain was a fine drizzle when Peter went back to the house after school on Monday. He crossed the muddy yard and was relieved to find the front door unlocked and swinging slightly in the breeze. Rain had blown into the hallway. There was no rush of warmth from the living-room as he opened the door. The fire was out, a heap of fine ash spilling over on to the hearth, and the usual smells were suspended in the chill air.

The birdcage was shrouded in its flowered night-time cover. Mr Briggs lay back in his armchair, his legs stretched stiffly in front of him, his mouth open. Peter was surprised that he was not snoring. He called his name softly. Then, since there was no answer, he tiptoed to the cluttered table and gathered up his case and his music-folder. "Cheerio, Mr Briggs," he said quietly. He left the cold, silent house, shutting the door behind him.

After his tea he went upstairs to his bedroom. He assembled the instrument and propped up *Daily Exercises for the Clarinet Student* on the bookshelf. He started to practise. A family of starlings chattered and complained outside his window. Before long his eyes were filled with tears and he had to stop to blow his nose. He started playing again. The third time the music came to a sort of gurgling halt, his mother wondered downstairs if perhaps the clarinet lessons were a waste of time.

AGNES OWENS

The Silver Cup

If you glanced in at Sammy's room when the door was open it seemed to be on fire. This was the effect of the flame orange paint which he had stolen from a garage. The room was really as damp and fetid as an old shed and contained a sagging bed, a set of drawers riddled with small holes caused by darts (not woodworm) and a carpet tramped free of its original pattern. Sammy liked his room. It was his territory and a haven to his friends who shared it with him most evenings from five to ten o'clock. The message on the outer panel of the door, "KNOCK BEFORE ENTERING", was directed at his parents. Sammy's Ma did her best to comply with it. His Da was inclined to kick the door open if enraged by the noise coming from within, but usually ordered his wife to "see what that bugger's up to", rather than risk raising his blood pressure to dangerous heights. Sammy's Da was not a happy man. He was banned from smoking and alcohol, was on an invalidity pension due to a poor heart condition from over-indulgence on both counts, and saw little in his son to give him pleasure. Yet pinned above the mantelpiece, the faded photo of himself when a youth was the spitting image of Sammy.

"Why don't you take your dinner beside us?" asked Sammy's Ma, entering his room with a tray of food after knocking.

"His face wastes my appetite," said Sammy sitting on the edge of his bed, wrapped in a multi-coloured sleeping bag, twanging his guitar. Sammy's Ma sighed.

"What a sight you look. If the cruelty man could see you —"

"Close the door behind you," said Sammy, his face invisible behind a fringe of hair.

Back in the living room she lifted her husband's plate the second he had mopped up the final trace of gravy with a chunk of bread.

"Going somewhere?" he asked with a touch of sarcasm.

"I think I've left a pot on the gas," she explained, dashing through to the kitchenette where she felt safe amongst the unwashed dishes. She focused her thoughts on the evening ahead. The western film on the television was not to her taste but it should keep her husband quiet. He always maintained he liked a bit of action, but none of that lovey dovey stuff, nor plays that were all gab, nor anything which related to female predicaments. Sammy's Ma had learned to keep her mouth shut about what she liked. After the film he was certain to go to bed with, as he described it, brain fatigue, prompted by "certain persons", whom she took to mean herself. Then, alone, she would sit through the remainder of the viewing, her eyes flickering between the clock and the set, marking time until twenty-past eleven when she would make herself a cup of tea. By half-past eleven she was back at her post, cup in hand, leaning towards the screen, all attention to the preacher on "Late Call". She considered his sermon as good as a tonic. If she closed her eyes she could imagine she was in church. Not that she ever attended church. Her husband viewed darkly any mission which necessitated her being gone from the house for more than an hour. Besides, her wardrobe was lacking in the formality required for such an occasion. "Late Call", brief though it was, gave her an impression of being part of a congregation listening and nodding in unison. Sometimes, in a more fanciful mood, she imagined she was sailing down the Mississippi in a steamboat while an invisible choir sang "We shall gather by the river", which was strange, since she had never been further than the townhead in all her fifteen years of marriage.

"Have you seen my good ball-point pen?"

Her husband's voice broke into her thoughts, causing her to drop into the sink a plate, which immediately cracked.

"Not recently."

She turned on the water forcefully to hide the ruined plate.

"I've looked everywhere!" he shouted.

Sammy's Ma shook her head in despair. His pen, his screwdriver, his socks, his heart pills, were just a few of the articles which he lost daily.

"Have you tried behind the clock?"

"Everywhere, I told you," then he added, "except that bugger's room."

"I don't think Sammy's in his room."

She had been dimly aware of a door slamming a while back, which could have meant anything.

"All the better," said her husband, and strode off.

Sammy's Ma suspected the pen was an excuse for him to search her son's room. Once he had found a heap of empty beer cans and a half-full box of potato crisps under the bed. "Thieving — that's what he's up to," had been his cry at the time. Sammy's staunch denials and assertion that one of his pals' uncle owned a licensed grocer's had not impressed her husband. She was placing the cracked plate in the bin when the roar came. When she entered Sammy's room her husband was holding aloft a large trophy in the shape of a silver cup. Senselessly she asked, "What is it?"

"What does it look like?" he thundered, pointing to an inscription on the base which said "PRESENTED TO THE PENSION CLUB BY COUNCILLOR HOOD". Sammy's Ma placed her fingers on her lips, unable to speak.

"He'll not get away with this," said her husband.

She sat down on the bed feeling giddy. To rob a pension club was unforgivable. A football club was more acceptable, when one considered the risks.

"He'll do time," her husband stated with satisfaction.

In a feeble manner Sammy's Ma said, "But he's not old enough."

"He'll go to an approved school then."

"Oh no," she whispered, while her husband peered inside the cup, saying, "This must be worth a few bob."

Blinking rapidly Sammy's Ma chanced the suggestion, "Maybe if you returned it there might be a reward."

His eyes bulged. "Me — return it?"

"You could say you found it in a field when you were out for a walk."

"The only place I'm returning it to is the police station," he replied, banging down the trophy on the chest of drawers.

Sammy's Ma almost bit through her lip. She could picture the neighbours in the street watching Sammy being led into a police van. They would snigger, and look up at her window, and shake their heads as if it was only to be expected. She knew they talked about her. Once from her kitchenette window she heard a woman in the back green say to another, "That one upstairs is a proper misery. Never has a word to say and runs along the road on her shopping errands as if she hasn't a minute to spare." She also knew they nicknamed her the road runner. Desperately she blurted out, "If Sammy gets lifted they'll only say we're to blame, and you most of all because you're his Da. They'll say —"

She broke off when her husband punched the wall in anger.

"Who'll say?" he demanded.

Sammy's Ma shrugged her shoulders and closed her eyes for a second. She had a great wish to stretch out and sleep on this sagging but quite comfortable bed of Sammy's and forget it all, but a groan from her husband snapped her to attention. He was rubbing the knuckles of his right hand.

"Are you all right?" she asked dutifully.

He sat down beside her breathing heavily. "I'm never all right in this bloody house."

Surreptitiously Sammy's Ma moved away from the proximity of her husband's body. She stared at the cup on top of the drawers. To her it had the look of a memorial urn on a grave. Moved by the association she suggested sullenly, "Perhaps we should bury it."

"Bury him is more like it," said her husband, lifting the cup from the drawers now with a proprietary air, and polishing it lightly with the cuff of his sleeve. He appeared calm and breathed normally. "Could be worth a few bob," he said again.

"I shouldn't wonder," agreed Sammy's Ma without enthusiasm.

For some moments her husband continued to polish the cup with one cuff then the other. Finally he cleared his throat and said, "Our Perry could do something with this."

"You don't mean he could sell it?"

"I'm not saying he could, but," he looked furtively towards his wife, "he knows all the fences."

"Fences?"

"Somebody who handles stolen goods."

"It wouldn't be right."

Her husband shouted, "God dammit woman we didn't lift it in the first place, but it's one way of getting rid of it with some money to the good!"

"I'm not bothering about money," said Sammy's Ma primly. "Besides, it will be traced with that writing on it."

Her husband wiped beads of sweat from his forehead. "Silver can be melted down," he said through clenched teeth.

To placate his mounting wrath she said dubiously, "I suppose it's not the same as stealing a purse, but all the same they'll miss it."

"It will be insured. They can get another one." Her husband jumped violently to his feet. The rebound from the sagging mattress threw Sammy's Ma across the bed.

"I don't care what you say!" he said. "I'm getting rid of this cup the best way I can, even if it's only to see the look on that bugger's face when he discovers it's gone."

He slammed the door hard as he left as if to shut her in.

Back in the living room Sammy's Ma looked down from her window to the street opposite where a group of women sat on the steps outside their flat, chatting and laughing and carelessly exposing their legs beyond the limits of decency. She clutched her husband's small bottle of heart pills, which she had found behind the curtains. She was thinking that for once she would have them ready on his command, when Sammy suddenly appeared.

"Who's been in my room?" he asked vehemently.

"If you must know it was your Da," she replied, placing the pills in her apron pocket.

"What? Why?" he queried in a high-pitched tone. She regarded him sadly, standing with arms folded.

"B-but," Sammy spluttered, "you know my room is private."

"Better tell him that."

"Where is he?" said Sammy, jerking his head about.

"Out." She added, "Seems he found a big silver cup in your room. Thought he'd better get rid of it. Thinks it's worth money, so he took it to your Uncle Perry. Appears he can get in touch with a fence."

When Sammy remained open-mouthed, eyes as usual concealed behind his fringe, unresponsive to the statement, she said, "Imagine anyone being called a fence."

"It's not his cup to get rid of," Sammy finally gasped.

Sammy's Ma sniffed. "It's not yours either. Donated to the pension club it read."

Sammy punched the air and shouted, "It was a pal who left it here! He was taking it to the jeweller's to get the inscription fixed! He just left it while we went out for a gang bang with the boys up the lane."

Sammy's Ma wrinkled her forehead. "Gang bang?" she repeated.

"What am I going to tell him?" demanded Sammy.

"Tell him it's probably being melted down," said Sammy's Ma with a nervous snigger.

For a second her son stood as if turned to stone, then he was out of the room in one long stride shouting, "He'll go to jail for this."

Two minutes later the sound of raucous laughter came from his room. Apparently Sammy's pals had a sense of humour.

She checked the time on the clock on the mantelpiece. It would be a long wait for her tea before "Late Call". She decided to waive the rules and make it now. In any case the prospect of the religious programme had lost its appeal after all this stimulation. She longed to speak rather than listen. At the window again she sipped the tea and noticed only three women emained on the steps. They no longer laughed. One yawned as if bored. The other two stared in opposite directions in an estranged manner. Clearly they sought diversion. Sammy's Ma became quite giddy with the notion that seized her, which was to join them on their steps. The story of the silver cup was too good to keep to herself. They would appreciate the humour and the irony of it. The difficulty lay in the approach, since a bare "good morning" or "good afternoon" was the most she had ventured to any of them. Then she conceived a great idea. She dashed into the kitchenette and quickly brewed three cups of tea, which she placed on a tray and carried down the stairs of her flat. She was crossing the street towards the women, flushed and smiling, when her foot caught on the grating of a drain close to the pavement. The cups shattered on the ground, followed by the tray. As she bent down to retrieve the one unbroken cup the pills fell from her pocket through the bars of the drain. Peals of laughter resounded in her ears like the bells of hell going tingalingaling as described in the song. But the mocking women were not unkind. Two of them arose from the steps and led her back across the street. They escorted her up the stairs to her flat saying, "You'll be all right."

"It's about this silver cup," she began when they pushed her gently inside the door.

"I must tell you about this silver cup," she said again.

"Yes, yes," they soothed, placing her down on a chair inside the living room, while they looked around furtively.

"I really must tell you about the silver cup," Sammy's Ma insisted.

"Do you think we should phone for a doctor?" one woman asked the other.

"Is your husband around, dear?" said the other to Sammy's Ma.

They decided to leave when Sammy's Ma began to laugh hysterically. On their way out they heard the discordant strum of a guitar from Sammy's room. One of the women tapped the side of her head significantly while she gave her companion a meaningful glance. Softly they closed the door behind them to create no disturbance, and tiptoed down the stairs.

153

The Snob Cross Incident

16 February

. . . it's not as if they're doing any harm . . .

18 February

. . . I suppose they've nothing better to do . . .

19 February

It's annoying, that's all. We always used to have a few of them standing around the take-away, but now we've got them all the time. Round the clock. When I wake up at three, and go in to check if Jamie's kicked his quilt off, I've taken to looking out of the front window. Just the street-lamps bleaching the sky; and them, half-a-dozen of them, on the pavement by the traffic-lights. Three in the morning. The traffic-lights go through in sequence, all the same.

Sometimes if they hear a car coming, far down the road, they press the button and bring on the green man. They can judge it exactly. The car stops, but they don't cross of course. Quite often the car drives through the green man signal, and then there's a burst of shouts and jeers. Just for a minute. I don't suppose it does any harm really.

I don't think I'll show this to Frank after all. It would worry him to know that I'd been worrying while he was away.

Not that I am.

23 February

There are more of them now. I counted thirty when I went out to collect Fiona and Jamie. They didn't stop me or anything. They didn't exactly move out of the way, though. I had to pick my way among them as if they were permanently fixed to the pavement.

So they are by now.

It's as if they're working in shifts. The girls are there in the morning, when I go down for milk and rolls. They're the cheekiest. I hear an echo sometimes as I leave the shop — "Thenk yeow. Mawnin'!" Is that really how —? Well, I'd rather speak like that than —

No. They haven't had the chances.

Still, they're cheeky.

The take-away has closed.

24 February
Definitely shifts. The big boys are there by four o'clock. I can't let Fiona and Jamie come home alone. It's bad enough for me. Not that they do anything, exactly. They're just there.

26 February
On the phone to Margaret, haven't seen her for months. She says she isn't going out much just now, doesn't like to leave the flat empty. Asked her why of course. Turns out it's the same on her side of town. It started three months ago, she says, and there have been break-ins. They know when people are in and when they go out.

I never thought of that.

Asked her why the police don't move them on. She says they just re-form across the road, or at the next set of lights. They can't be pinned down. Also they outnumber the police. Over the whole city, she reckons, at least fifty to one.

Over the whole city?

I never thought of that either.

1 March
Have been phoning around. It's true, they're all over. Anniesland, Shawlands Cross, Battlefield. Thirty, fifty at a time, aged twelve to twenty or so. Not doing anything, exactly. Break-ins beginning, can't quite be pinned on them. The green

man trick has just turned up in Shawlands. Judith, over in Battlefield, says yesterday they started breaking telephone wires. Casually, she says, to pass the time.

2 March

Tracy looked in this morning en route for her mother's. Said she got lost in the East End and found herself at Bridgeton Cross. I asked if crowds of youngsters there too. No, she said, none at all. Amazed to see the crowd here. Haven't they got homes to go to, she said? Yes, I said, but no jobs of course. Suppose not, she said. Terrible, she said.

It was very bad at four o'clock.

Late shopping night so I asked Mrs D upstairs to sit with Fiona and Jamie. Drew extra from the cash machine and went to the supermarket. Bought two of everything on my usual list. Pure panic buying, I've never done it before. Bought things I could hardly believe when I unpacked at home. Candles, crispbread, long-life milk. What in God's name am I preparing for?

At four o'clock there must have been fifty of them. Fiona, Jamie and I had to worm our way through. I wanted to push and kick. I'm sure some of them began to follow us upstairs. I turned round and there was a scutter and a giggle, nobody to be seen.

Came home with my huge shopping-bags, waited to hear Mrs D safely in her flat, then shut and bolted the storm-doors. Seven o'clock at night.

Wrote a long letter to Frank. Told him we were all well but counting the days till he came home. Crossed out *days*, put *weeks*.

It's more like three months in fact.

Damn, I'll have to get to the post-office tomorrow.

3 March

Decided to post my letter in town. You hear of lighted matches thrown into pillar-boxes. That would be their sort of thing.

Picked up more shopping too. Books, toothpaste, torch batteries. (*What* am I expecting?) Long wait for a bus home, panicked in case I'd be late collecting the children. Bus finally came, packed with grannies on off-peak tickets. Strange feeling aboard the bus. Talk of how unusually long bus took to come, how unusually glad everyone was to get it. As if it was the last there would be.

Strange conversation on the top deck. Two or three youngsters jumped on ahead of me, didn't pay, went upstairs. I followed, as lower deck full of grannies. Heard one youngster say to another, "Where are you today?" Answer: "Snob Cross." "Me too." They got off at my stop and joined the crowd.

I'd forgotten all about Snob Cross. We're Cobhill Cross of course, a very good address, tree-lined residential streets, convenient all amenities, as the ads say. Snobhill Cross was what the bad boys called it in primary school, Snob Cross for short. Haven't heard the name since then.

Snob, terrible term of insult in Glasgow and district. Joke (true): Guidance teacher berating boy, calls him among other things a slob. Boy loses head, shouts will get faither up, nae right callin me a snob. Teacher, bemused: Wait a minute, I didn't say snob, I said slob. Boy: Oh, that's all right then.

Snob Cross. Convenient shops, schools, bus routes.

It's very quiet tonight. There aren't half as many buses as usual.

5 March

I'm quite sure now. They gather at the Snob Crosses. West end, south side, middle-class areas, white-collar, traditionally *employed*. Doesn't always hold true now, but they don't seem to take account of that. Not Bridgeton, but Shawlands. Not Glasgow Cross, but Cobhill Cross.

There aren't even so many cars about. The crowd spills over on to the street. They cross back and forth as they like. Toss bottles of milk from hand to hand. Naturally some fall and break. Haven't seen a road-sweeper or a bin-lorry for days.

Haven't seen a postman for days either.

Two policemen walked past on the far side of the street, trying to look as if everything was normal.

6 March

When I came home with Fiona and Jamie there was a big dent in the storm-door, just at the lock. They hadn't got in, quite.

Went to the window and looked down at them, sitting on the pavement with their milk-bottles and rolls. No wonder the dairy's always running out of things. I saw the big black-haired boy who's always there at four o'clock. He looked up and saw me. I know him and he knows me. I know he's there at four o'clock. He knows I'm always out about then. I don't know what to do.

Went up and talked to Mrs D. We rigged up the old baby-alarm with the microphone in my flat and the speaker in hers. I don't know what she could do if she did overhear a break-in. I don't know if the police would even come.

Tried to phone Tracy later. Couldn't get through. Tried Margaret, same result. Looked out of the back window, saw a telephone wire dangling from the pole.

Looked out of the front window. The black-haired boy saw me and grinned. I went back to the kitchen and began to cry. Frightened the children, and didn't help at all.

9 March

Dairy closed. Deliveries haven't come for two days. Heard the woman saying to one of them, "It's you, nobody will come near because of you —" They said, "Us? We're no daein anythin." I bought the last half-dozen eggs and went upstairs. Later I heard the dairy's windows being smashed.

Coming back at four o'clock nearly impossible. They're everywhere. Sitting in closemouths, scouting about the back courts. Got an evening paper. Newsagent putting shutters up. Doesn't think he'll open tomorrow.

Paper says what everybody knows now. Cobhill, Annies-land, Shawlands under siege. Buses diverted. Cars garaged, those that haven't been overturned. People prisoners in houses. Well, that's true. Can't let Fiona and Jamie go to school tomorrow. Can't face them again.

Reporter brave enough to ask them, what's it all about? They quite pleased to be asked apparently. Forgotten generation, they say. On scrap-heap at sixteen. Got to make people take notice, they say.

But it isn't my fault . . .

The black-haired boy is sitting on our front wall. Sees me at window, grins, looks at his watch. Sorry, son. I know it's late shopping, but I'm not going out tonight. I've got eggs and sardines and long-life milk. I'm not going out at all.

Have bolted the storm-door. It's only five o'clock.

10 March

School problem solved: schools have closed. Extra in-service training, TV says. Closed till further notice. That's all I heard before TV went fuzzy. They haven't got up to the aerial surely?

Lights blinking oddly too. Electricity sub-station down the street. But they'll fry themselves if they mess about with that.

Worth losing power and light for, maybe?

But no, they'll just pull a switch somewhere. They'll march in and take over. There are so many of them. They don't do anything — Well, nobody can prove it —

The afternoon shift is coming on. Bringing provisions. They smile gently and touch hands. There's far less shouting than there used to be, far less mischief and noise. When they do something now it's quiet and it's major. They know they're in total command.

The black-haired boy lifts his milk-bottle to me and drinks deep. We're out of milk. Two eggs left, the children can have those tonight. The lights are certainly dim.

It isn't our fault.

It isn't fair.

12 March

I saw two policemen across the road, but too late to call out.

159

13 March

Fiona and Jamie are so bored. Keep asking for crisps, which are finished of course. Insist on looking out of the window, not a good idea, but haven't the energy to make a scene. Anyway no violence outside, no orgies. Their voices murmur on. Sometimes they sing.

I saw policemen again. Almost sure it was the same time as yesterday. Maybe there's a chance?

14 March

Must try today in case the routine changes. Have asked Mrs D to come down at half-past three. Will tell her I've heard there's a crate of milk coming in. If I'm down there by quarter to four, I should see the policemen, if I'm right about that.

I've got to be right.

The big boys will be there by then, but it can't be helped.

* * * *

UNEDITED VT OF OUTSIDE BROADCAST, TV NEWS AT NINETEEN, 14 MARCH

REPORTER: This is Cobhill Cross in the west end of Glasgow, where earlier today a young man was taken to hospital with severe lacerations and suspected internal injuries. A woman is reported to be helping police. Residents of this pleasant tree-lined residential district —
VOICE OVER: (blows raspberry)
REPORTER: Residents of this pleasant, er, popular tree-lined area see today's incident as the climax of a campaign of harassment by young unemployed people. Mrs Davidson, you live at ninety-five Cobhill Road?
MRS DAVIDSON: I wish you wouldn't give my name and — Well. Never mind.
REPORTER: I believe you've had a lot of harassment from these young people?
MRS DAVIDSON: Well — yes — no —
BOY'S VOICE: Hi there, Mrs Davidson, ninety-five Cobhill Road, two up right —

VOICE OVER: For God's sake tidy this up before it goes out —

REPORTER: The young people themselves take a different view —

GIRL: Lost the heid, so she did. Comes oota her close and dives at Kevin. He tries to get oot the road, right? She goes for him, teeth, nails, you name it, knocks him doon, an then she —

VOICE OVER: We can't use this —

MRS DAVIDSON: It wasn't like that at all! She shouted to me, told me, she was trying to get to the police, that boy wouldn't let her past, it was the last straw —

VOICES chant, a wordless jeer, drowning her out.

MRS DAVIDSON: It's your fault. She'd never have —
 (To REPORTER)
 It was all because of them —

REPORTER: (hastily) Tony Barker, News at Nineteen, Cobhill Cross, Glasgow.

BOY'S VOICE: (blandly) Us?

A. L. KENNEDY

Star Dust

The first snow fell tonight; this evening. There's something about it being there, outside; the soft, wavering shadows against the glass. Inside, however you were feeling, as soon as you realise snow is here — the first snow again — you get better, you feel snug.

I wanted to open a window tonight, to put my hand outside into the weather and let the flakes tickle on my palm. In a few hours, there will be rain, or sleet, or something and, by morning, what I see will no longer be new. People will no longer walk through a different country, strange and careful, as if they were being watched. I should keep this as it is. I should take a photograph.

Sometimes I am asked to say why I started taking photographs and I tell them, because my daughter bought me a television set. If I were younger, that would make them puzzled and they would ask me to explain, but now, of course, they smile because I can't have understood them and then they leave and tell each other I'm confused.

But the truth is that I did start taking pictures when my daughter sent the television set. I had never wanted one — never in my life; books and the films and radio were always enough for me, but still, she sent me one, even though I told her not. Didn't I have to stare at one for fifteen years, perhaps longer, and don't I know by now what I do not like? In any case, it came in time for Christmas and in the New Year, it would be company for me.

It was company for someone else, because I sold it. The January papers were filled with unwanted gifts and I didn't

162

get the price I might have done. I wasn't worried. The camera that I wanted was quite inexpensive and, even buying film and a cleaning kit, I found I had a deal of money left. Some of this I spent on photography books, because borrowing them from the library wasn't enough and I needed to know about filters and lenses, exposure times and depths of field. I love these words. These words are lovely. They are happening now, they are young words, and because I understand them, part of me can still be happening now and young.

Still, I always buy the *TV* and *Radio Times* and study them for Susan's sake, so whenever she phones I can talk about the programmes I don't watch. But she doesn't often ask.

How do I really explain about the photographs? Unless I say that television pictures can't belong to me and can't be a special occasion that could please me like the cinema and so my daughter's offer made me discontented. Or, at best, it made me realise how discontented I was, because I have always wanted pictures that would be mine and that would keep a hold of special things. Things like the first snow.

A woman in my position, I know, shouldn't need a camera. All my momentous occasions have happened, apart from my funeral and I won't be taking any pictures there. I haven't even got a family or loved ones to photograph: Archie's been gone for years now and Susan lives in London with a man I hardly know.

London. That doesn't seem fair. While I was younger and fit for it, we never had the money to go there and, even with the money, we couldn't have found the time. We would never have thought. Now, travelling is faster and doesn't, I suppose, cost quite so much and certainly, I've plenty of time, but my health has gone and I couldn't face the journey. I got down twice on my pensioner's card and it seems that'll have to do, but it makes me feel, somehow, cheated; dissatisfied. And I don't have any record of when I was there. Not one picture of the baby with me there, too.

My possible subjects are certainly limited, now. I imagine that people like me would tend to have fewer close relatives and most of our friends would tend to be dead. So, there's nobody left to take pictures of but strangers and ourselves when the papers tell me that strangers and old ladies shouldn't mix and, at no time, have I ever been a beauty. Not bad in the face, but no tits. I never used to say that word, but nobody seems to mind now and neither do I. I lost a lot of weight in my twenties and your tits are always the first things to go. Not even having Susan altered that. In any case, even if I'd got the chance, I wouldn't have wanted pictures of myself.

It's funny, I do have some snapshots from one time I went away, but I would rather I had nothing left at all. If I think of all the films I went to see: Garbo, Dietrich, Veronica Lake, Bogart and Spencer Tracy, even Ronald Colman: the films they made are just as good now as they were when I saw them new, but those two little pictures a stranger took of Archie and me look as if we're dead and buried, years ago. We haven't kept well.

Me and Archie should have been a film. A woman at the bowling club told me that her nephew had appeared on television. Four years ago, this was, before I had the fall. He was in a quiz, apparently, with prizes and they brought him down to London with his wife, paid for their room in a lovely hotel and sent them on a guided tour. She said she took a video of the programme, but what's the point? He'll be on for a couple of minutes, be made to look a fool and that'll be it. He didn't win.

By now, they'll all have done it. They're nice enough people, but I know what they're like. They'll all have gone off and done something, just to keep up. The last time I was there, it was getting on the radio. That was the thing that everyone had to do. They asked for dedications, or called up and gave their opinions, or answered questions. There were quizzes then, too. You couldn't explain it was nothing, only noises in the air. Nice enough people, like I say.

I have come to the conclusion that I deserve better things, that's all. I know I'll not get them, but that's fine. I would rather be content in hoping and making my position clear than settle for lies and nonsenses and second best. I will take pictures of the things which are important so that I can keep them to look at again and, one day, I will maybe make a film.

When I couldn't go out to bowl any more and I hadn't thought of photographs, it turned out that I started watching films at the cinema. I am very lucky in where I live; once I've got down the stairs from the second floor, I have only to walk round the corner and the supermarket's right there. I can make the Botanic Gardens on my better days and, behind me, there are grocers and bakers and the whole of the Byres Road, right down to Partick. I also have my pick of two cinemas. The both of them seemed a bit shabby, which is why, I think, I'd never gone before, but, one afternoon, I was already out and I started feeling tired and then, along with all the other poor souls, I was drifting into the pictures, really, for the sake of company.

That time it was Robert De Niro, whom I'd already seen in something with my daughter in Leicester Square. He was very good. Here, they changed the features almost every week and the one place had a choice between two films, because they'd cut the screen in half, to make two small ones, and, of course, I went back after that; I got very keen.

You'll believe me if I tell you, but you won't understand, that when leaving your home for a pint of milk has to be planned in advance and you know you won't bump into friends while you're out, because most of them are dead, it tends to throw you back on yourself. You either get dottled, or you think a lot, or sometimes both.

It seems strange to me now that our painters and our poets and novelists aren't all of them sixty-five and over. How could you get the time to think and imagine properly when there's people and money and children and things going on? I don't know how they manage it when they're younger. I suppose they must just want to do it very much. I do know I have to want to do it very much, or end up like Mr McShane at the Tuesday Club, who spends half of his time in Spain in the Civil War and the rest of it talking to chairs and feeling himself. I don't want to die in public in a hospital, or some institutional lounge where I've dragged around for years, forgetting myself and smelling more and more of my own piss. That clingy, awful straw and

165

honey smell of stale piss. The Tuesday Club at the Centre is thick with it. If you say pensioner to me, it's the first thing that comes to mind.

There are brighter things to think of, though. For instance, I make a point of remembering past events, because I want to be sure that I always know what's happening and what's now. If you practise that every day, you can tell the difference. I make lists of bills and shopping to keep myself straight and then, when I've done my exercise, when I've proved all the cogs still fit, I can put a cassette into my player and I can start imagining.

You have to be very careful when you imagine and you're alone. Some people I've seen have locked themselves up in their heads and swallowed the key. They can't get out. Even when it seems you're doing fine, you can slip into wishful thinking so easily. I must have spent months in the Spring and Summer just after my fall, running through what I would do at the bowling club. Several of the ladies and the couples have cars and all of them offered to come and take me down there, as soon as the season began. I wouldn't be able to do much, they realised that, but I could sit at the side and watch them; enjoy the crack. They said it would be company for me. I was silly and looked forward to it all — what I would wear, the rugs and thermoses needed, what a sharp observer I would make. Naturally, nobody came. I haven't seen one of them since.

Now I'm careful with my thinking. Going to the cinema helps; it gives me ideas. Particularly, Robert De Niro gives me ideas.

I look at him, and the other ones like him, and they spend so much time and energy on just looking ordinary. There are lights and backgrounds and special effects and music; that's a very important thing; and all of this is there to make them look better than ordinary. They want to look everyday. When Meryl Streep wakens up in a film, she'll want to look as if she's been to sleep, only, she'll seem much more wonderful, because films look at people so nicely, they can't help seeming wonderful. I have an idea that the ordinary people should be in the films. They wouldn't have to waste their time forgetting they were stars and they would get their chance to be wonderful. This means that I now spend some of my thinking time imagining films for people that I know. Sometimes, for people that I love. The best one is my mother's film. That's the best one of all.

My mother was two different people, one of them is hard to remember, the other one I've only heard about. If I'd been older when I knew her, I could have understood her more, but you always miss the best of your mother with only being a child while she's there. I only knew she was a mixture of things.

When she was alone, or thought she was, you would sometimes hear her singing in her birdy, pipey voice. When I heard it first, I thought it was someone outside, or a stranger with her, and then I got to our door and the music stopped and, when I looked in, there was nobody there but her. She didn't have a face you'd think would sing, there was something wary in it, something closed, but that day in the room, even when she had stopped herself and was hiding her song away, there was still a glow about her. It was slow to fade. That was the first time I wondered what age she was.

I always knew it was her when she sang after that; whether the words were strange ones in Gaelic, or springy ones you'd heard whistled in the street. I would try sometimes to be quiet and still on the stair and wait to listen to her through the door.

The only other times I saw that shine about her came when she told me stories she made up. My father might take the boys out on a Sunday and, if he did, there would just be my mother and me alone and, if it had been a good day, there might be a story for me when I asked. She spoke about a country full of names I couldn't say which had animals and mountains and was never too far from the sea. I think now, she was telling me her childhood and that was why it often made her sad.

Her sisters, when I met them later, told me she always sang when she was young. They described a light, laughing woman, who had danced until her cheeks and forehead flushed and who either cried because she was too happy, or because she had a daft, soft heart. The woman I remembered was older and pale with concealing a sickness that no one else could reach. At meals, she served herself the smallest portion and barely took a peck from out of that. She saved up her tears for the washhouse, where they could join sweeter waters and my father wouldn't see.

Mother died when I was eleven and left me with the man who had eaten up her joy. He made me understand her weeping and the noises that had wakened me in the night. I wouldn't make a film for him. All that I want to recall of him is I'm glad of the way he died and couldn't have prayed for better, or been more satisfied. Drunk at his work, he crushed his hips to nothing under a girder. And other people told me, so it must be true, that he squealed and screamed for hours before the end. I think of him in that wee ambulance, leaving the yard, and it makes me think less of myself, but I can't be sorry.

For my mother, I've thought of a film where she could be happy. This one could have launched her in her new career and recorded just a little of her joy. I have made it a Gainsborough film, with that lovely, faded kind of colour that would have been more comfortable for her eyes. The story would remind you of Jane Austen, but the dresses would be prettier. Mother would wear dozens of them to sing and play, to dance in brilliant candlelight, or to walk across lawns of emerald green and fall gently and deeply in love. Her hair would be long and, when it was freed, it would shine, it would light in her eyes. People who had never met her would all agree how beautiful she was and, instead of disappearing when I die, she would be part of us; a star. That would be no more than she deserves.

My films are only silliness, I know, but I enjoy them and they help me set things right. I want there to be something to say I was here; that all of us were here, and that sometimes we have felt we were discontented. If I could be the first pensioner film director, I would make films about us. I wouldn't choose anyone special, like a spy, or a general, who might be remembered, or famous for anything else. I would film an ordinary person, their story, because they have good stories, too. Someone should remember them. I don't think the public would feel they'd been disappointed. In fact, because of the way that films make you look at things, I don't think they would notice a difference.

Even I have a story. It wouldn't be one that I could use, I'm not so proud of myself as that, but if somebody would film it, it would be good. I would like to leave something behind me to say that the dottled old woman who walks on two sticks and shows slides to the Tuesday Pensioners' Club, did have a story. Things happened to her.

The film would have things to explain. I hear the young women in the Centre where they hold our club and I think they live in harder times than we ever did, but if I showed them how it felt to eat and sleep and cook and wash and mark off the years of your children and your living in the one square of a room, maybe they would wonder why there hadn't been a bigger change since then. I know I never had time for such thoughts when I was younger. I wasn't angry that I lost two babies, only glad my little Susan thrived.

My children had a father, of course, to share the room; a good man who worked hard. Tam. He took me away from my father and brothers which only a good man would have done. We had to move north of the river after that and leave our friends behind. I hardly ever saw Tam drunk and he never hit me, he was tender in his way, but I hated him. I hated all the hours spent with the two of us penned up in that room. I hated myself for using him to get away from another room and, at night, although he was gentle, I hated the smell and the touch of him. Now, my father would have got the jail for what he did to me, but what was done would still have been done, and I would still have been the way I was. Tam believed that I was shy.

We did the thing that films always want you to do; we moved into a wee bit better place and, slowly, we could feel more safe. Tam was a painter to trade and, although the quality customers went elsewhere, he built a business for himself. By the time the other painter was in Poland with his troops, Tam had three men on his books.

I met Archie when the war was two years over and Tam was busy setting up again. Archie wasn't fair. The first time we were properly alone together, it was a winter afternoon. Dusk was falling and he took my hand in the street and made me stop. He looked up.

That's the first star, Margaret, you should make a wish.

He knew that wasn't fair. He knew what I would wish.

The film would show how easy it is to be unfaithful to a busy man and how easy it is to want something beautiful. It would show me my happiness. We would be singing as Archie drove his car out past Milngavie and his arm would be round my waist as we walked in the grass. A low, dry stane dyke had fallen away on a slope and he stepped across the flat spread of stones. My shoes were a little slippy, unsuitable, and he reached his hand down to pull me up. That would only be a tiny moment in the picture, but it would show our hands and faces and be slow and watch the way that people choose things they'll remember. I could tell you how warm the sun was, that the breeze smelt of the morning's rain and which birds sang. It made me cry — that one movement he'd made without thinking. It told me too much about him, too suddenly. His grip was too sure and gentle. His strength was too reliable. He felt as if he might be a giving man and as if he might care. I had never wanted to meet the right man for me. I had never had the space for hopes like that and then Archie made me feel he had finally come when everything was all too late.

I told Tam I was poorly and I needed some time to myself. He didn't mind; he would take care of Susan. He imagined I was going to a friend in the country. I took a taxi to the railway station and Archie met me there with his car. We stayed in a little hotel away in Argyll and for four days I was Mrs Sturrock and not Mrs Mackintosh.

I wouldn't want to show our love. I never saw it, because my eyes were closed. I heard my voice in a strange, close bedroom, telling him about my father, I told Archie everything. I woke up each of the mornings, wanting to look at him. I wanted him to be still sleeping so that I could watch his face and wake him when I snuggled up because I liked touching him. The last morning I cried. We told the young man at reception that I was feeling unwell when we came down with our cases and I was so pale. We said it would be better if we just started off for home. He smiled.

Tam never believed a word of it when I told him. He was a very settled, confident man, so he couldn't believe it. It almost made him laugh. I seemed to disappear when he was like that. I was so used to him being right, it was very difficult to be sure that he was wrong. I had to keep the picture of Archie very clear in my head. In the end, there was nothing left but for Tam to be angry. Susan was in from school; she was nearly seven, then, and his shouting brought her in from her room. She looked white and worried and we shouldn't have sent her away again so upset, but we did. And when she had closed the door, Tam told me that, in any case, of course I would never leave because, if I did, I wouldn't see Susan again.

The next day I wrote to Archie in a letter I didn't send. I told him that I loved him, which I hadn't said before, and then I tore it up. I tore it up and didn't send another and, when I was meant to meet him next, I didn't go. I hope he understood, but I think that it's far more likely that I hurt him and he hated me, which is a shame because I did love him. He never tried to get in touch.

So, I stayed with Tam and Susan and life was sometimes uncertain and sometimes comfortable. My daughter got into a nice school and learned to be different from us. I waited and, when I was fifty-three, Tam died. Susan came back from London for the funeral. It was good to have her stay here for a while.

I think I would finish my film with the funeral, because there isn't much that happened after that. What there is seems very personal, anyway, as it happened when my time was all my own. I don't know if I'd want it seen in public. Increasingly, there seem to be only tiny patches in my life that are at all important. There are images, or moments, more than anything bigger. It's material more suited to a series of photographs.

CARL McDOUGALL

A sunny day in Glasgow long ago

1

The library was dark, cool and quiet. Here and there sunlight slid across the books and gathered on the russet parquet flooring: little dust dots bounced around.

There were blue white and gold ragged cornices and ceiling ornaments, chandeliers with frosted upsidedown goldfish bowls like moons round a big brass planet and long velvet curtains folded maroon in the shadows. There were little pine desks, each with a reading lamp, chairs and room for four. There were wee women with shopping bags, old men with sticks, girls who smelled of summer, young men with their sleeves rolled up. A girl in a long Laura Ashley dress stood in an alcove reading someone's poems. She shifted her weight from leg to leg, haunch to haunch. As she moved the light sparked in her hair.

For a time I'd been lost in the book, but now there was a big happy sigh somewhere inside. I'd expected an urge, a rush of blood, a nervous jump, but all I got was a smile inside, a bubble and a sigh.

I started to read at the top of the page: *Plashwater Weir Mill Lock looked tranquil and pretty on an evening in the summer time. A soft air stirred the leaves of the fresh green trees, and passed like a smooth shadow over the river, and like a smoother shadow over the yielding grass. The voice of the falling water, like the voices of the sea and wind, were as an outer memory to a contemplative listener; but not particularly so to Mr Riderhood, who sat on one of the blunt wooden levers of his lock-gates, dozing. Wine must be got into a butt by some agency before it can be drawn out; and the wine of sentiment never having been got into Mr Riderwood by any agency, nothing in nature tapped him.*

2

I put the book on the shelf and left the library. The detector buzzed as I passed and a librarian looked at me. When I stopped she smiled and said, It's okay.

In the foyer my eyes adjusted to the sunlight. I stood at the door, beneath the canopy, watching a wee man at the foot of the steps. He was shouting about Jesus, a nervous wee man, grey in a grey suit. He wore a sign like a tunic. The front was written in big black letters and the initial letter of each word was red: THE WAGES OF SIN ARE DEATH. The back said REPENT in red, NOW in black. He waved a Bible and walked up and down, speaking in patches.

When the last trump is called and the sinners stand naked before their Maker crying on merciful Jesus to save them, where will you be? Will you be in the heavenly host with God and the everlasting blessed or will you burn in the fires of Hell with your women and your drink? Will you turn to the man who died on the cross? Will you repent? Or will you suffer the torment of the damned, the anguish of the sinful, the torture of the unredeemed.

O wee man. Wee man.

3

The men were taking a stroll before going back to do something important. They walked in twos or threes, hands behind their backs; suits, ties and nicely polished shoes.

The girls were on an hour's holiday. They giggled, posed and chattered, aimless and released; a happy sight, all bounce and sway and summer.

4

In the Square an Army band was playing a selection from *The Sound of Music*. They finished Climb Every Mountain with a fine flourish. Some girls shouted: Give us the Slosh. The conductor saluted and announced a selection of well-loved Scottish melodies.

As the full band belted out the first few bars of Roamin in the Gloamin an old man in a torn raincoat and cap climbed the barrier round the bandstand and gave us a sand-dance. When the girls cheered the conductor swung round, saw the tramp and smiled. The old man goose-stepped to Tangle o the Isles and started shadow boxing when they tilted into Scotland the Brave.

Two policemen opened the barrier and led him away as the piece ended. The girls booed and the conductor saluted, some strollers were applauding. The conductor switched on his microphone. Thank you Fred Astaire, or should I say Muhammed Ali. He laughed heartily at the crowd who were watching the policemen chase the tramp across the Square, then announced a selection from Our Favourite Westerns.

5

All around the Square were little groups of people. Girls on the grass with skirts drawn tightly round their knees or sunbathing with cardigans across their legs. The lads laughed too loudly; they lay on their stomachs and stared at page three or straight ahead, searching.

Some kids played tig round the war memorial; others were cowboys on the backs of the blind docile lions at the memorial entrance.

On a bench beneath the memorial someone was sitting on a newspaper listening to the band.

6

Back to the library, dark and cool and quiet.

I read a little but couldn't concentrate. I imagined a hill, fresh snow and a trail of young trees climbing beyond me towards the sun.

I sat in the library a long long time.

7

The Square was quieter now, the band gone and the strollers back at their desks. Grass was bent, darker where they'd been sitting; papers, bags, cans, cigarette packets, clumps of trash scattered across the grass and round the Square. Flowerbeds had been disturbed and broken privet branches tilted awkwardly beside the fountain.

The sharp smell died when the bus came. I was alone in the cool upstairs breeze, a skewered heart drawn on the seat in front.

> *Creepy the Gam says everythings nice*
> *Vambo rules this pitch and all others*
> *Young Tiny Tiny Muggy never never die*
> *OK yous moonmen*

We stopped in a dull canyon. Summer clothes looked strange in the shadowed light. The doors swung and we lurched forward into the sun.

8

The sun was shining on a still afternoon. I put my jacket over my arm and wandered down a quiet street. The park would be busy, but quieter after teatime. And it was going to be a lovely evening.

FARQUHAR McLAY

Thresholds

I

They were sitting in the back-room of the Burnt Barns, a low-amenity, winos' dive in the last of the Calton slums. They had been there for two hours and it was now 7.30 p.m. Kandy sat at a battered old piano with a newspaper spread out in front of him. From time to time he sipped his whisky and turned a page. Albert sat at a side-table close by, smoking a cigar and observing his friend. The only other customer in the back-room was Olga. She was on a stool at the bar talking to Eddie the barman.

"What about London?" said Kandy, without looking up.

"I thought you'd had it with London," Albert said.

"Yes, but I'm stronger now."

"So what did we get passports for? We're going to Spain."

Kandy ran a hand through his hair.

"Well, let's just see what the money's like first."

"The money will be okay, believe me."

Kandy bent low over his newspaper. The two men sat without speaking for some minutes, then Kandy laughed and said: "Would you believe it? Here's somebody got three years for nicking sausage skins."

Albert rose and pushed Kandy's glass towards him.

"Come on, drink up, I'm on the bell."

Kandy watched closely, an amused look on his face, as Albert went to the bar. Albert whispered something to Olga and she threw her head back and let out a shriek of laughter which shook the gantry.

When Eddie came with the order he beckoned Albert a little to one side. He placed the drinks on a small steel tray and drew from his hip-pocket a large, official-looking document. He unfolded it and flattened it out on the bar. The two men pored over the document and spoke in whispers. Now and then Eddie got quite agitated and waved his arms about.

It was a performance Kandy had witnessed many times. In the Barns people were always showing documents. It was usually a citation or a summons to appear before this or that court or tribunal. Sometimes it was a notice of rent arrears, and other times a notice of eviction. Sometimes it was a notice of distraint for the poinding and repossession of goods. Sometimes it was just a letter from the DHSS or a pawn ticket. It didn't matter what it was, nobody had penetrated the Barns unless someone at sometime had shown him a document. Nobody had ever shown Kandy a document. The thought made him smile. The Barns folk had their suspicions of Kandy. He was either a cop, a grass or a queer. They didn't like the look of him, whatever he was. They assumed Albert was only using him.

When Albert came back with the drinks, Kandy said: "I'd like to know how you do that. I'm more of a prole than you are and I can't get near them. They're in the palm of your hand. I mean, why should Eddie, who wouldn't trust his own mother, trust you? And what did you say to Olga to make her scream like that?"

Albert re-lit his cigar.

"They're my friends, Kandy."

From Kandy's wide-open mouth came a staccato hiccup of a laugh. He raised his glass.

"All hail Albert — friend of the dinosaurs!"

"Is something troubling you?" Albert said.

"Troubling me?"

"Yes. You sound troubled."

"Well, you're right. I am troubled. Why aren't you?"

"I'm thinking about Spain."

Kandy folded up his newspaper and threw it down on the table in front of Albert.

"I still think I'll try London."

"You've tried London. You had to come back."

"Sure. But that was long ago. I've changed. Things will be different this time."

Albert picked up the newspaper.

"What makes you think you've changed?"

"Well, I'm older now, for one thing, more mature. Plus the fact: this time I'll have money. Even you will agree that can make all the difference. But it's this feeling I have. I feel the old self-confidence coming back."

Albert opened out the newspaper.

"That's good."

"You know something, Albert, I acted too hastily in giving up teaching. I should have listened to my headmaster. I should have listened to my doctor. They gave me good advice. Give it time, they said. Think of your pension. Think of your mother, it'll break her heart. But what about me, now, I said, I'm disintegrating. And I was. I had lumps springing up all over my body, my hands, my face. I was coming apart. But I should have waited. I should have stuck it out. If I was in that school now, feeling like I do now, I'd win through. It was a bad bloody school, right? A bad locality. Children without hope, going nowhere but the dole queue and knowing it. And what the hell did I know? What kind of crap was running through my head? I would bring them hope: I would open up their world. And they just laughed, and they —"

Kandy's voice rose with his anger almost to a shout.

"— unruly, stupid, malicious little brutes — they shat on me!"

Olga looked round and Eddie, hands in the sink under the bar, fixed Kandy in a sour and truculent stare.

Kandy smiled and subsided. Under his breath he said: "I think your friends hate my guts."

"They don't," Albert said.

"Why do you keep dragging me in here? You know I can't stand the place."

"It's better than chrome and plastic."

"It's the people, damnit. They hate me."

"You're wrong. They don't hate you. They just don't know you. You should come in more."

Albert rocked back slightly on the two hind legs of the spindly plain chair. He held the newspaper opened out at arm's length. Kandy said: "Do you think I'm stronger now?"

"I notice you never count your change," Albert said. He lowered the paper and leant closer to Kandy. "They could be giving you anything back, you never look. In fact, you turn your head away. You do. It's almost as if you were ashamed: as if you didn't really believe you had any right to anything back. That's the impression I get, anyway. Of course it could be you just trust people."

Kandy shook his head.

"I don't trust people."

At that moment Olga went into another loud laughing fit, apparently triggered by something Eddie had said. She swung round, bent double with laughter, lurched from her stool and made in the direction of the Ladies. Eddie was leaning across the bar nodding his head mirthfully. When the toilet door slammed shut, Eddie, still beaming, cupped his hands over his mouth and called out to Albert: "She's peed her knickers, silly fucking cow."

Albert made no acknowledgment, just stared straight ahead, as if not hearing. Eddie quickly gathered himself up and busied himself at the gantry. Kandy said: "It's a matter of temperament, that's all. I may be a well man again but I'm still me. You're you. I don't have to become an exact replica, do I? You have your way of dealing with people, I have mine. Your way suits you okay. My way suits me."

"You're like a man with a blindfold, Kandy. What frightens you? What can they do to you?"

Kandy rested his elbows on his knees and stared down into his drink and said nothing. Albert got up.

"Never mind, Kandy. You'll find yourself again — once we get over there. This time tomorrow it'll all be different. This place and all the rest forgotten. You'll see."

Kandy looked up anxiously.

"You're going already?"

Albert tapped his watch.

"I've stayed too long. We don't want any mistakes, do we? have to be certain where she is."

"Listen, Albert — sit down a minute."

"No time."

"One more drink before you go."

Kandy made to rise, but Albert, passing behind him, placed a hand on his shoulder.

"Give me about an hour. You're sure you've got the address?"

Kandy looked about him forlornly and nodded.

"I've got the address."

Albert went to the door.

Kandy said: "I can get drunk in an hour."

Without looking back, Albert said: "You do that."

II

When, one hour later, Kandy arrived at Rina's house, the front door was lying ajar and he walked in and closed it quietly behind him. The hall was a long passageway lined with barometers, some were of giltwood, some of mahogany and some doubled as clock and barometer. Two other clocks, nine-foot grandfathers with massive brass dials, stood, niched like sentinels, on either side a doorway through which he could see Albert pouring drinks into paper cups.

"I picked up a wee carry-out on the way up here," Albert said. "It's a dry house, you see."

Kandy strolled round the room. In a long display case bracketed to the wall he could see masses of silver cutlery, tankards and plate. A tall rosewood vitrine scintillated with a thousand glass objects: there were enamelled vases in etched cameo glass, blue opaline glass caskets, silver-mounted glass ewers, gilt glass goblets, smoky grey lalique mice and cranberry dragonflies.

"What do you think of all this?" Albert said.

Kandy threw out his hands in a bewildered gesture.

"It's incredible."

At the far end of the room, occupying a Georgian bookcase, was Rina's collection of Meissen and Royal Doulton figures. Kandy stopped in front of the bookcase.

"There's a few quid there," Albert said, giving Kandy his drink. "You're smack on target."

Kandy took out his glasses and peered at the figures. He pursed his lips and nodded, like a connoisseur.

"Of course. Of course. I can tell quality when I see it."

Albert smiled.

"I wasn't talking about the porcelain."

He slipped a key from his pocket and unlocked a drawer in the bookcase. He drew back a tangle of beads, brooches, necklets and bangles, to reveal several thick layers of banknotes.

"How does that grab you?"

Before Kandy could speak, Albert had snapped the drawer shut again, locked it and pocketed the key.

"That's the prize," Albert said. "The thing is: you don't take the prize with a key. It's ours — yours and mine — but we can't take it with a key. If we want that money we'll have to break the place up."

Kandy sipped his drink and turned away.

"You never mentioned that part."

"You want out of this dead town, don't you? What's a little vandalism?"

"Christ, she's your aunt. She brought you up."

Albert moved towards the vitrine.

"If you start on the porcelain, I'll attend to the glass."

Kandy took up a little iron-red dish.

"You said it was just junk."

"So what would you call it?"

"I can see it's not junk."

"No, you can't. Remember what you're supposed to be. Weak, stupid, brutal, spontaneous. Like your ex-pupils, the no-hopers. They shat on you. Think what they would do here."

Kandy put down the iron-red dish very gently, with both hands.

"She'll know it was you."

"Will she?" Albert said.

"Somehow she'll know."

Albert was leaning against the vitrine with one hand, his head lowered. In a quiet voice he said: "Yes. Yes you're quite right. She'll know."

Both remained silent for a time. Then Kandy lit a cigarette and said: "I know you want to make it look like a break-in. But honestly I don't think she'll go to the police. I can't see her doing that. Not if we just take the money. Mind you, if we start smashing the place up . . ."

"We have to. Everything has to be smashed. There's no other way."

Kandy finished his drink and went to where the carry-out stood and poured another. Without looking at Albert, Kandy said: "You want her dead."

"Dead?"

A slow, sad smile broke on Albert's face. He went to Kandy and led him by the arm to the mantelpiece. Before them stood a gold-framed photograph of an unsmiling woman of about thirty with a small boy at her knee.

"What can you read in that face?" Albert said.

"Is that Rina?"

"That's Rina. And the misbegotten little runt beside her, that's me. Look at her face. It has a robbed look, wouldn't you say? The worst has already happened to Rina."

"How?"

"Years of saying no to everything. Even summer. When the sun shines Rina hides. She refuses even summer. It takes a long time for that look to work itself out in people. You have to live with refusal a long time before you look like that. You have to be in hiding all your life. Too many summers lost. That's what's happened to Rina."

Kandy had taken the photograph in his hands and was studying it closely.

"You have a kind of robbed look about you yourself."

"They left me with her when I was eight. They didn't want me and they didn't want each other, so they dumped me on Rina. Nobody even said goodbye. I remember there were some hymns and a few prayers, and that was it. They'd gone. My life with aunt Rina had begun. She had money, this nice big house, and nobody in her life except the Lord Jesus. She was the ideal choice. Except for one thing: Rina preferred things to people. Nice things that don't wet the bed or vomit their dinner on the carpet. Quiet things that don't jump up and answer back, or fly into rages and throw themselves down and beat their fists on the floor. Chaste little dears without a single filthy longing in their pure little hearts. Nice and quiet and chaste and safe — that's Rina's world. Everything safely locked up in a glass case."

"But not you?"

"Yes, me too. It took a while, but I learnt to become what Rina wanted. It wasn't easy. But I bear no grudges. Not against Rina. Not against my parents. In fact I'm quite pleased with my parents. They let me off the hook, they set me free."

"And Rina won't, is that it?"

"Rina can't. It's more like I have to free her."

Kandy replaced the photograph on the mantelpiece.

"I still don't think she'll call the cops."

He turned to Albert.

"But that's not really what it's all about, is it? It's not even about the money."

Albert shrugged and said: "We have to forget all that. We can examine motives later, if we feel like it. At this moment we're vandals, robbers, nothing more. We must just accept that. We have to do as they would do. Why should we pretend we're different? There's no nice way of being a vandal and a robber — a desecrator. We'll desecrate. And we'll take the prize when we get to it."

The two men faced each other in silence. Kandy went pale and he looked down at his hands and they were trembling. He slumped down on a chair by the fireplace.

"I'm not sure I can do it, Albert."

"But there are other rooms. This stuff is everywhere, all through the house. I need your help."

"I didn't think it would be like this."

Albert went close to Kandy. In a whisper he said: "And there's upstairs as well."

"Upstairs?"

"Oh, yes. Upstairs. Rina's bedroom. We can't neglect Rina's bedroom."

"Will there be time?"

"If you help."

Kandy looked down into the cold hearth.

"Where is she anyway?"

"At Hebron Hall, with the Brethren. It's just along the road. That's her church. They have Jesus there. A very pretty, docile little Jesus."

III

The two men lay side-by-side, Kandy's head in the crook of Albert's arm, blankets and coverlet heaped at the bottom of the bed.

"Talk to me about my mother," Kandy said.

"Why should I? You chose me."

"But you don't realise how sick she is. She's dying. She needs me."

"And who does Kandy need?"

"How can you be so hard, so cold?"

"When we choose life people say we're cold."

"You sacrifice nothing."

"What makes you think your mother wants a sacrifice? Maybe it's your sacrifice that's killing her."

"She cries at night. Every night. She turns her face to the wall and cries. I lie listening. What did I do wrong, Albert? What was it, all those years ago? Sometimes I think I once knew, when I was stronger, when I could face it. But not now. It's gone now. It's buried. But not for her. Some awful betrayal, some act of treachery she can't let go of. And all she can do is cry. And I can't help her. Nothing I say or do reaches down into that pain."

Albert raised himself on one elbow and looked down at his friend.

"You can help her. When we're in Spain she'll let go."

Kandy smiled. He raised his hand to Albert's cheek and kept it there.

"What a great simpleton you are!" Kandy said.

"None greater."

"Don't worry. I know it's only a game."

"Yes. But we make things happen."

"Then make it happen for me. Tell it to me again. I want to hear it all again. I want to believe it's true."

Albert covered Kandy's hand with his own.

"When we're in Spain your mother will let go of her hurt. Better things will take its place. She will forget, as Rina will forget. Betrayals, treachery, lies — all will be forgotten, and forgiven. They suckled us only with their delusions. We can deprive them of their delusions. And more than that. We rid them of guilt, because we now cease to be occasions of guilt. We take up their burden of guilt on to our own shoulders. We carry it into the light where it'll shrivel up and die. You chose me, and I chose you, for no other reason. And is it not possible that they may even go beyond forgiveness, and piece the whole thing together, and feel towards us finally only a sense of the sincerest gratitude?"

A little later the two men left Rina's house separately, as they had come, and met up again in a small hotel near the centre of the city. The following day they caught the first flight out to Spain.

WILLIAM BRYSON

The Tip

A high mound of rubbish is arranged in the centre of the dump. Rotting food and rags of clothing escape from burst plastic bags. Discarded consumer durables; washing machines, smashed television sets and radios spew out their own entrails. Yesterday's newspapers flap old troubles in the wind. Torn magazines and books lose their pages which blow down from the top of the mound.

An old man sits at the foot of the mound barely distinguishable from it, wearing a dark suit. The old man is reading a newspaper in the dawn. He finishes the paper and looks towards decaying tenement houses, which seem to slope down into the dump. He takes a watch from his pocket and looks closely at its face — and then looks again. He waits.

When he looked up again Hough was standing with his back to him, looking towards the tenements. A hand grasped the neck of the wine bottle jutting from the pocket of the overcoat. Hough turned from the houses and stared at the old man, the wind bringing water into his eyes.

Hough moved over to the old man, sat beside him. The old man held the watch in the palm of his hand, held it under Hough's face, with a grin; but Hough kept silent, sipping from the wine bottle. When he had finished, he said, "Old Man," and gave the bottle. He thrust the hands deep into the pockets of the overcoat as the wind burnt his face.

"This watch was working when I found it," said the old man, "the hands were moving. When I wound it up, to keep it going, the thing stopped, the hands stopped moving."

It was then that the old lady came to them, bundled up in a dirty black coat. Clasped to her chest like a baby was a doll. She released it from her, held it out to Hough; she looked towards Old Man, as if pleading. Hough was silent. "Vic," said Hough and gave the bottle into the hands. She sat to drink, placing the doll on the ground by her side, leaning against the plastic bags.

"I got lost last night," said the old man. "I walked and walked till I came to this long road. So I walked for miles and miles. At first there were houses at the side of the road, but after the first mile there were no houses. So I walked on and on.

"Before the end of the road it was dark. At the end of the road and down a grass mound was a motorway. The cars reached it by moving down a ramp. All the cars were moving lights across the motorway. Well I never had a car, I don't have a car, so I just turned back.

"After the first mile my daughter Jane and her husband Ken came up in the car. It's a Ford Cortina, new registration, automatic and all. We were the only people in the road, it was dark, like, all around. The light from the car just shone on us. They took me into the car, put the blanket they keep in the back around me. All the way back they gave me silence.

"My daughter she said to me, like, she said that I needed to have a bath. I said I thought I had a bath yesterday but this watch is stopped. How can I tell if I don't know the time? Ken said we've got plenty of clocks — you can see the time. No, I shouted, that's your time how can I tell my time from them clocks, yours . . . I can't tell the time from them.

"So they gave me a bath, Ken did. He stripped me of my clothes, then when I was in the bath, he washed me, like I was a little baby. I told him I thought I'd had a bath yesterday, but that I couldn't keep a hold of time because my watch had stopped. I must have got the days mixed up. Well, he said, don't start that again. Then he dried me."

"Last night," said Hough, "my wife, Pam, she got the children ready, she made them put on their coats. Then she got bags and plastic bags and things. The telly was on but I still listened. But she never said anything. She talked into the phone and ordered a taxi; I listened and heard her say our address.

She waited with the kids quiet, then she must have remembered something and went into another room to find it.

"I was left with the children, but they were quiet. I was embarrassed, I don't know why. I looked at the telly, but I looked at the children as well. They looked sad, as if they were about to burst into tears, I looked at the telly, I turned away, I looked at the children, they were silently crying.

"Then Pam came in. She got out a handkerchief, she wiped the children's eyes, she did it very hard, as though she hated their tears. They waited quiet for five minutes till the taxi came."

"Was it a private taxi, what kind of car was it?" asked Old Man.

"No, it was one of them black jobs. Then they got in the taxi and went away," said Hough.

"Where'd they go?" said Old Man.

"I don't know. I waited until the telly finished, but they never came back. So I turned the telly off."

"The other day," said Old Man, "I had a whole bottle. The grocer's at the corner. You know the street, it's that shop, blue it's painted. I drank the lot myself. Then I walked about.

"I went into the launderette, it was the only light in the street. I went in, said hello. I don't remember how many people were there. I sat and watched the clothes go round and round.

"Then the people told me, beat it, move it, get to hell. I told them wait till the clothes have finished. They said you never brought any clothes in. I said you go and find your own clothes to watch, I was here first, I've been watching these all night. They said we're going to get the manager. I said he's not getting watching either.

"So the manager came, she said, if you don't get out I'm calling the police. So then I ate the soap powder."

"Last night," said Vic, "I went to my daughter's house. Lovely it is. Garden, front and back door — two children — she's got the lot. I stood at the gate, I looked at the house, the flowers in the garden, lovely. I breathed in the air coming from the garden — refreshing.

"I stand there and wait for them to come out. They're in, I know, the light is on.

"It gets cold. I can't wait long I thought, it's getting too cold. It gets colder but still I watch. I forget, so I look at a photograph I have of them so I'll know them when they come out. I keep waiting. I've got them in my mind's eye now. I wait a long time but it's worth it.

"I told Mrs Martin, I told her I'm going to my daughter's. She said that's nice. I say she's making me my tea, she's setting it all out.

"Look! I show her the presents I bought my grandchildren. Mrs Martin said how old are they now. I tell her Paul's three and June's five. She said June must be at school now.

"I said I can't go up to the house until six because they'll be working. She said what about Paul. Nursery I said.

"Mrs Martin tells me, she said have you heard about Maggie. I said no. I said Maggie who. She tells me Bob Malcolm's wife. I said what. She said heart attack yesterday. I said no. She said sixty-six.

"So I wait outside the house and think I'm sixty-five years old, it makes you think. And then the lights go out. I look again, the light did go out. I wait, perhaps they've just forgotten. So I wait. But they don't come out.

"So I walk home in the dark. I drop one of the presents, I'm too tired to pick it up, too tired. I walk home in the dark."

Old Man, Hough and Vic were silent as they watched the trucks roll into the dump. They ran up the long paths toward the mounds. The trucks headed toward the south mounds making noises like beasts.

Some of the dustmen jumped from the trucks to watch the drivers unload the rubbish. It all tumbled in a mess, come from the suburbs like faded gifts, presented to no one in particular.

When one truck had finished delivering its waste, another would take its place and begin the process again. There were four trucks today. Tumbled out the rubbish, on and on, as if for ever. At last the trucks had coughed up everything.

With their work done, the men stood around and talked. Old Man, Vic and Hough couldn't hear them from where they

189

sat, but they'd heard it all before. The men used swear-words
to complain about the filthy backcourts they had to clean, about
one of their members not doing his fair share of work. They'd
heard it all before.

The men would talk about things they had done the previous
night; went to this pub, saw this film, watched this programme,
met this girl. The men would talk about the weekend coming,
what they were going to do with their money, what they were
going to buy. They'd heard it all before. The men told jokes,
they laughed ... they told more jokes, they laughed some
more.

They waved their lit cigarettes like wands as they spoke, as if
they had to say magic words before they could leave. The men
talked, the men left.

Up the paths went the trucks, with the men clinging to
their backs, up into the distance, until the men could be seen
no more.

Old Man, Hough and Vic took their time; they might go over
later, it didn't matter, they were old hands. It was best to wait,
let the air into the lungs, let the brain cool, keep time in its
place. If they waited the sun might make an appearance. Keep
hope, have heart. They were together, they just weren't talking;
they had run out of words. The sun would thaw them out; have
hope, keep heart. They waited and the sun got stronger ... it
could make the day.

Hough passed the bottle around, the sun was bright on the
liquid inside. They would have a drink and then go over. The
sun brought out the smell of rotting vegetables.

"Come on," said Hough.

Across the mud and garbage-strewn tip they walked, across
the light of the sun, across to another mound. The mound
was larger than the one under which they sat, but that was the
only difference. They stood before the mound for a minute
when they reached it, their eyes looking up and down. Fingers
moved a piece of rubbish here, a piece there, like a surgeon
diagnosing. All separated to do their own thing.

The wind escaped from the sun, the sun hid among some
clouds that were passing, ashamed; it got dark. Pages fell

from the top of the mound, torn randomly from their books; Old Man collected the torn pages and tried to put them in some sort of order. He held the paper in his hands, worked hard putting the paper in sequence, ever and ever, on and on; but the wind puffed out its cheeks, blew all the harder and the pages flew from Old Man's hands and the sun hid all the more.

Paper rode on the wind, blew around the mound to Vic, but she ignored it. She moved some rubbish and it fell to her feet. Ever and ever, on and on she worked, among old crisp packets, old useless metal, burnt wood, colour magazines and broken toys; it all fell to her feet, some sort of liquid wet her legs. Some black plastic bags fell, burst open to reveal their contents and then Vic would search through them; but she never opened a bag if it was closed. She searched ever and ever but there was nothing.

Hough looked, he didn't know what at, but he knew there was something to see; he walked, he waited. He got colder, the hands pulling the coat closer to the body. He walked to keep warm, still watching, searching for something. A cough racked his body, blood came in his mouth. He spat some out, swallowed the rest. Something metal fell from the mound, he walked to get it. Keys! He jingled them in his hands; some of them were twisted, some of them rusted. Hough looked around, looking for something they could open. There was nothing and the sun hid all the more.

Vic and Old Man came round to Hough's part of the mound. Old Man held the pages under Hough's face, Vic showed her empty hands; Hough held up the keys, jingled them. They shivered. Hough passed the bottle, they had a swallow of the liquid inside. The wind burnt their faces. "Come on," said Hough and they made their way back to the mound under which they sat.

"You know," said Hough, "I would sit before the telly, I would see it all; all the killing, all the hate, the wounded, the dead, I would see it all. The children running from the wreckage, from the bombed buildings, from the guns and from the baton-charge. See the tears falling, the children and old women crying, see it all in colour; the rivers of tears and blood.

"And then I lost hope for my children, had to run away from them — they were so weak, how could I help them against all that?

"You see Pam and me we got married so we could have children, a house, a life of our own, but then when we got them, when we had them, I wanted love as well. I wanted the sun, not an electric bulb.

"Pam told me, she said you've changed. She said when you go out to work tomorrow don't come back, but where else could I go? Every night I watched the bloodshed, I wanted to cry but how could I in front of the children and how could I help them if I wasn't allowed to be human?

"I tried to make sense of what was happening but there was never a moment's respite. Pam said you don't care anymore, what the hell happened to you. I tried to talk to Pam, to the children, but I couldn't shout above the bombs and the crying. I was too weak to shout."

"If only this watch would start," said Old Man. "When I was working you needed a good eye for time. When I was working in the factory you needed a good eye for it. To know when to clock-in, to know when to go for dinner, to know when to go home. You needed a good grasp of time, it was essential. I was never late, I made sure I knew the time all the time. I had my eye on the clock, on a watch, I could tell you the time any time of the day.

"Up at four every day, when it was dark outside, quiet-like so the children slept; but my breakfast would be ready, the wife was up before me to make it. We both had a good knowledge of time, it helped us to bring up the children. When to send them to school and when to make time to help them in troubles."

"When my daughter left me," said Vic, "my heart stopped beating. It was going well, beating even when I was sleeping, but when she left me it just stopped.

"I went to the doctor, told him all about it, he listens for about a minute then gives me some tablets. They're not real tablets, they don't give you real tablets any more. They're called placebos and made of sugar, they're pretend tablets. That's why people don't get better anymore, they're not getting medicine.

My daughter didn't just leave me, she left me for ever."

"My wife went to the doctor," said Old Man, "then she went to the hospital, then I don't know what happened to her. I never saw her again."

"Did she come out of the hospital again?" asked Hough.

"No, I waited outside, hours and hours . . . never came out, no." Old Man covered his eyes with his hands.

"Did you go in and ask the nurses, the doctors, what happened to her?" said Hough.

"I knew to wait, so I just waited."

"Was she dead, was that it?" said Hough.

"Yes that was it." Tears fell from Old Man's eyes; Hough realised he had driven him too hard, that Old Man hadn't really wanted to talk about it. He got the bottle from the pocket to give Old Man a drink — it was empty. Although broken bottles spilled glass over the tip, Hough put the bottle back in his pocket. Yes, that was it, he thought. Keep heart, have hope. Yes that was it and the sun hid all the more. They waited for the sun to come out.

"I'm going back to that house," said Vic, "I'm going to wait outside until they come out. I'm going to wait and wait more and more."

Hough got the bottle from his pocket. "It's empty," he said, "I don't know if I can get more."

"I'll wait," said Vic, "that's what I'll do."

She pulled the coat closer to her body, walked with her head down, through the tip, overcast by dark clouds.

"She left the doll," said Hough.

Old Man and Hough waited for their brains to fill up with words so they could speak again. Hough walked around the mound; when he came back to Old Man he had a wooden packing-case. Old Man and Hough sat; Hough on the packing-case, Old Man in the dirt. They waited for the sun.

Wind blew pages from the top of the mound and Hough caught some in his hands. He looked towards Old Man, held the pages under his face. He spent time trying to put the pages in order, working hard with Old Man watching him. When he had finished, he looked towards Old Man again.

"Let's get the books up there."

"It's too high."

"But look, we can stand on this, can't we?" Hough stood with the packing-case in his hands. "You can give me a leg-up."

"I'm too tired," said Old Man.

"Come on," said Hough.

They placed the packing-case against the black plastic bags, stood nervously together on its slatted wooden surface. Old Man cupped his hands together, Hough placed a foot in them. His hands grasped a plastic bag above his head, the weight in Old Man's hands. Before Hough could climb, the packing-case gave — its surface broke under his and Old Man's weight and they both fell through. The plastic bag Hough had touched fell on to them, bursting and spilling its refuse over them.

Old Man and Hough wiped their clothes.

"You got more on you than me," said Hough. Inside his coat he could feel the warmth of blood running from his body; broken glass was all that remained of the bottle.

"I hurt myself there," said Old Man.

Hough didn't hear him, he was examining the packing-case, its splintered wood. He noticed writing on the side of the case. He looked towards Old Man, showed him the word "FRAG-ILE" stencilled in green. "It was fragile," he said.

Hough put his hand inside his coat, felt the blood from his stomach run over his fingers. He asked Old Man to move some plastic bags, to make a hollow inside the mound, so he could lie and sleep.

When Vic came back at dusk he still lay there. Hough rose from the plastic bags; he sat and looked at Vic, but his strength failed and he fell back again.

"I didn't wait," said Vic.

Notes and Acknowledgments

WILLIAM BRYSON (b. 1964 Glasgow) published his first story, "The Tip", in *An East End Anthology* (Clydeside Press, 1988).

MOIRA BURGESS (b. 1936 Campbeltown) edited with Hamish Whyte a previous collection of Glasgow short stories, *Streets of Stone* (Salamander Press, 1985). She has written a number of short stories and two novels, *The Day Before Tomorrow* (Collins, 1971) and *A Rumour of Strangers* (Collins, 1987). She compiled the standard bibliography of Glasgow fiction, *The Glasgow Novel* (Scottish Library Association/Glasgow District Libraries, 2nd edn. 1986) and edited an anthology of Scottish women's writing, *The Other Voice* (Polygon, 1987).

"The Snob Cross Incident" appeared in *New Writing Scotland* 2 (ASLS, 1984).

SUSAN CAMPBELL (b. 1961 Glasgow) was brought up in the Highlands and Skye and educated at Glasgow University. She has written short stories and film scripts. Her stories have appeared in *Short Story Monthly*, *Edinburgh Review* and *Original Prints*. A collection, *The Wreck and Other Stories*, is due from Polygon.

"Agape" appeared in *Original Prints* (Polygon, 1985).

DOUGLAS DUNN (b. 1942 Inchinnan) has published numerous books of verse, of which *Elegies* (Faber, 1985) was awarded the prestigious Whitbread Prize; his latest collection is *Northlight* (Faber, 1988). His short stories have been collected in *Secret Villages* (Faber, 1985).

"Mozart's Clarinet Concerto" appeared in *Secret Villages*.

RONALD FRAME (b. 1953 Glasgow) has published three novels, *Winter Journey* (Bodley Head, 1984), *Sandmouth People* (Bodley Head, 1987) and *Penelope's Hat* (Hodder, 1989), and three collections of short stories, *Watching Mrs Gordon* (Bodley Head, 1985), *A Long Weekend with Marcel Proust* (Bodley Head, 1986) and *A Woman of Judah* (Bodley Head, 1987).

"Incident in Le Lavandou" appeared in *A Long Weekend with Marcel Proust*.

JANICE GALLOWAY (b. Ayrshire) lives in Glasgow and teaches in Ayrshire. She has had short stories and poems in various anthologies and magazines, including *Chapman, Edinburgh Review, Margin, New Writing Scotland* and *Radical Scotland*.

"Paternal Advice" appeared in *West Coast Magazine* no. 3 (1989).

ALASDAIR GRAY (b. 1934 Glasgow) has published three novels, *Lanark* (Canongate, 1981), *1982, Janine* (Cape, 1984), and *The Fall of Kelvin Walker* (Canongate, 1985). His short stories have been collected in *Unlikely Stories, Mostly* (Canongate, 1983) and *Lean Tales* (Cape, 1985) in which stories by James Kelman and Agnes Owens also appear.

"The New World" appeared in *The Fiction Magazine* vol. 6 no. 2 (1987).

ALEX HAMILTON (b. 1949 Glasgow) has collected some of his stories in *Gallus, Did You Say?* (Ferret Press, 1982; also available as audio cassette).

"Car Sticker" appeared in *The Glasgow Magazine* 4 (Spring 1984).

JAMES KELMAN (b. 1946 Glasgow) has published three novels, *The Busconductor Hines* (Polygon, 1984), *A Chancer* (Polygon, 1985), and *A Disaffection* (Secker and Warburg, 1989). Collections of his short stories include *Not Not While the Giro* (Polygon, 1983,), *Lean Tales*, with Alasdair Gray and Agnes Owens, and *Greyhound for Breakfast* (Secker and Warburg, 1987). He edited *An East End Anthology* (Clydeside Press, 1988).

"Forgetting to mention Allende" appeared in *Greyhound for Breakfast*.

A. L. KENNEDY (b. Dundee) describes herself as a born-again Glasweigan. She has recently had stories in *Stand Magazine* and *Behind the Lines*, and in the anthologies *Original Prints 3* (Polygon, 1989) and *The Devil and the Giro* (Canongate, 1989).
"Star Dust" is previously unpublished.

FREDERIC LINDSAY (b. 1933 Glasgow) has published three novels, *Brond* (Macdonald, 1984), *Jill Rips* (Andre Deutsch, 1987) and *A Charm Against Drowning* (Andre Deutsch, 1988) and is working on a fourth, *Separate Cells*. He scripted *Brond* and *Jill Rips* for TV and is working on a film script, *Gilhaize*, for EBS.
"Die Laughing" is previously unpublished.

LIZ LOCHHEAD (b. 1947 Motherwell) is a poet and play-wright who also performs in her own revues and performance pieces. Among her publications are *Blood and Ice* (Salamander Press, 1982), *Dreaming Frankenstein* (Polygon, 1984), *True Confessions and New Cliches* (Polygon, 1985), and *Tartuffe: a translation into Scots* (Polygon, 1986).
"Phyllis Marlowe: Only Diamonds Are Forever" appeared in *True Confessions*.

CARL McDOUGALL (b. 1941 Glasgow) has published two collections of retold folk tales, *The Cuckoo's Nest* (Molendinar Press, 1974) and *A Scent of Water* (Molendinar Press, 1975), and his short stories have been collected in *Elvis is Dead* (Mariscat Press, 1986). His first novel, *Stone Over Water*, was published by Secker and Warburg in 1989. He has edited an anthology of Scottish short stories, *The Devil and the Giro*, published by Canongate in 1989.
"A sunny day in Glasgow long ago" appeared in *Prosepiece* (Pavement Press, 1979).

LORN MACINTYRE (b. 1942 Argyll) is a freelance writer and lives near St Andrews. He has published three novels in his Chronicles of Invernevis series, also short stories in maga-zines and anthologies and a collection of poems about Charles Rennie Mackintosh, *From Port Vendres*.
"Black Cherries" appeared in *New Writing Scotland 5* (1987).

FARQUHAR McLAY (b. 1936 Glasgow) wrote for the BBC in the 1950s and 1960s and has published short stories in magazines and anthologies, including *Streets of Stone*. He edited the Glasgow anthology *Workers City* (Clydeside Press, 1988).

"Thresholds" appeared in *New Writing Scotland* 6 (ASLS, 1988).

MAUREEN MONAGHAN (b. Glasgow) after many years as a teacher gave it up to open a small restaurant with her husband. She has had stories in *Scottish Short Stories* (1987) and *The Other Side of the Clyde* (Puffin Books, 1986).

"Saturday Song" appeared in *The Other Side of the Clyde*.

MICHAEL MUNRO (b. 1954 Glasgow) has had short stories in *New Writing Scotland* and *The Scottish Cat* (AUP, 1987). He is the author of the best-selling guide to Glasgow language, *The Patter* (GDL, 1985), and its sequel, *The Patter — Another Blast* (Canongate, 1988).

"Application" appeared in *New Writing Scotland* 4 (ASLS, 1986).

DAVID NEILSON (b. 1953 Glasgow) is author of *XII from Catullus* (Mariscat Press, 1982) and illustrator of Michael Munro's *The Patter* (GDL, 1985). His writing has appeared in *The Glasgow Magazine* and *New Writing Scotland*.

"In the Desert" is previously unpublished amd is from a work-in-progress, *Robert the Vole*.

AGNES OWENS (b. 1926 Milngavie) has published two novels, *Gentlemen of the West* (Polygon, 1984) and *Like Birds in the Wilderness* (Fourth Estate, 1987). Her short stories are collected in *Lean Tales* (Cape, 1985).

"The Silver Cup" appeared in *Lean Tales*.

DILYS ROSE (b. 1954 Glasgow) has had stories in many magazines and anthologies and on radio. A collection will be published in October 1989 by Secker and Warburg.

"Child's Play" appeared in *The Glasgow Magazine* 5 (1984/85).

ALAN SPENCE (b. 1947 Glasgow) collected many of his stories in *Its Colours They Are Fine* (Collins, 1977; reprinted by he Salamander Press, 1983). He is also a playwright and currently finishing a novel.

"Heart of Glass" appeared in *Scottish Short Stories* (Collins, 986).

EDDES THOMSON (b. 1939 Ayrshire) is a poet, short-story riter and critic. Publications include *Identities* (Heinemann, 981), an anthology of modern West of Scotland writing, and *he Poetry of Edwin Morgan* (ASLS, 1986).

"Harry Houdini in Cowcaddens: 1904" appeared in *A.M.F. Magazine* 4, May 1980.

ALERIE THORNTON (b. 1954 Glasgow) has had stories nd poems published in many magazines and anthologies, icluding *Cencrastus*, *Chapman*, *The Glasgow Magazine*, *New Writing Scotland*, *Scottish Short Stories* and *Streets of Stone*. A book n window-boxes will be published by Canongate in 1990.

"Crane Diver" appeared in a slightly different form in *Graffiti* (1984).

AMISH WHYTE (b. 1947 Giffnock) edited the best-selling nthology of Glasgow poems *Noise and Smoky Breath* (Third ye Centre/GDL, 1983; 5th printing 1988; 2nd revised edition orthcoming), and *The Scottish Cat* (AUP, 1987). With Moira urgess he edited *Streets of Stone* and with Simon Berry, *Glasgow bserved: A Documentary Anthology* (John Donald, 1987). He has lso published collections of verse. He is co-editor of *New Writing Scotland*.

"Berth" is previously unpublished.